# Winky Studmire
## And the Accidental Time Machine

G.T. Wiley

**BYRNE**
PUBLISHING LLC

ISBN: 1-62199-011-7
ISBN-13: 978-1-62199-011-6

# CONTENTS

Prologue.................................... 5

**Chapter 1:** The Slickster 1000........................ 7

**Chapter 2:** A Trip to the Dump..................... 24

**Chapter 3:** A Tragic Loss............................. 33

**Chapter 4:** A Change in Plans........................ 43

**Chapter 5:** The Building Begins..................... 50

**Chapter 6:** The Genie's Wrath....................... 58

**Chapter 7:** Trial Run.................................. 69

**Chapter 8:** A Shocking Reaction..................... 79

**Chapter 9:** The Accidental Time Machine.......... 85

**Chapter 10:** The Prehistoric Swamp.................. 95

**Chapter 11:** Frozen in Time........................... 104

**Chapter 12:** The Chase Begins........................ 111

**Chapter 13:** Trapped................................... 120

**Chapter 14:** Inside the T-rex........................... 132

**Chapter 15:** The Makeshift Battery Charger......... *140*

**Chapter 16:** The Original Residents of Mystic Bay... *149*

**Chapter 17:** Into the Future............................ *156*

**Chapter 18:** Frozen for Good.......................... *170*

**Chapter 19:** Betsy to the Rescue........................ *181*

**Chapter 20:** Home...................................... *192*

# PROLOGUE

It started out as a quiet weekend in Mystic Bay.
Off on the horizon, a storm was slowly building.
Huge clouds soared toward the sun only to be slashed
by the jet stream. Residents of the small resort town
took refuge indoors. The anvil-shaped cloud was
heading in their direction.

This would be no ordinary storm for Winky
Studmire and his sidekick, Slick Parker. What started
as a rather uneventful day would soon turn into one
of their greatest adventures. If only Slick hadn't
spotted the ad in the Mystic Times. If only the boys
hadn't gone out to the Mystic Bay Sanitary Landfill to
gather junk. If only Scooter, Mystic Bay's pet beagle,
hadn't been able to locate Milo Snitzer's old bus
batteries. But all of that happened as the storm
clouds approached, and then hovered over Winky's
garage.

A few hours later, and a few hundred million years earlier, a series of loud thuds startled Scooter from his hiding place under Winky's left armpit. The little flea-covered beagle poked his head up from between the two boys and barked a warning to Winky.

"Easy, Scooter, I heard it, too," Winky said.

"What made that sound?" Slick asked. "Whatever it was, it has to be nearby. I could feel the vibrations."

"I'm not sure what it was," Winky said. "Maybe our time machine is acting up." He went back to work on the transformer with his screwdriver.

Finally, Winky succeeded in slowing the spinning fan blades down to a crawl. "Look, I've almost got us stopped. The sun is barely moving now." He smiled in triumph. "This screwdriver is great! It makes a perfect control lever."

Slick gave Winky a congratulatory slap on the back. "I knew you could fix it."

Just then, the booming sounds began again. The wagon bounced a little higher with each vibration, as the sounds grew increasingly louder.

Something was headed their way.

***

Visit **www.winkystudmire.com** to see Winky's accidental video of this terrifying moment.

# Winky needs all the help he can get!

*You* can be a part of solving Winky's mysteries, comment on real photographs from his adventures, and start your own conversation with Winky and Slick! "Like" Winky Studmire's Facebook page, and then invite your friends to join in on the fun.

## *Be a part of the action at:*

# WinkyStudmire.com

For more G.T. Wiley books, visit

# www.byrnepublishing.com

# CHAPTER 1
## *The Slickster 1000*

"Go up to your room until you can walk through my house without breaking something," said Winky's mom. "That was your grandmother's favorite umbrella vase."

"It was an accident," Winky explained. "If I could go back in time, I'd move it away from the banister, honest."

"Time travel? You've been watching too much television," Linda muttered as she carefully picked up the broken porcelain. "What exactly are you working on up in your room? You aren't planning a trip back to yesterday, are you?"

"No, I'm working on my entry for the Electric Car Competition," Winky said. "But someday time travel *will* be possible," he predicted. "And I just might be the first one to do it."

"I'm sure you will, dear," said Linda, half listening to her son as she finished her task at hand.

"Can I take those broken pieces upstairs?" Winky asked. "I'll glue them back together and paint over the cracks. You'll never know that I broke it."

"Don't bother," Linda said. "Wait until your father sees this."

The doorbell saved Winky from another lecture on the proper way to come down the stairs. In a flash, he disappeared back up the stairs to his bedroom before his mother could stop him.

"Oh, hello, Slick," Linda said when she opened the front door. "What are you planning to break?"

"Break?" Slick said, and then looked around the porch to see if he accidentally stepped on something. "Um…Is Winky here?"

"He's upstairs working on a car or a time machine, or something. Who would know?"

"I know; he showed me his blueprints." Slick stepped inside. "I can't wait! I've always wanted to ride on a dinosaur."

Linda raised an eyebrow as Slick bolted up the stairs.

Slick didn't stop running until a bedroom door separated him from Mrs. Studmire.

Winky's bedroom was amazing. A double window provided a panoramic view of Mystic Bay and the harbor. Beyond the sheltered harbor was the Atlantic Ocean.

A double bed accented the far wall. Next to the bed was an entertainment center. It housed a television set with five speakers mounted on the ceiling. The subwoofer hid on the floor under Winky's bed.

Despite this sweet setup, the boys spent most of their time on Winky's computer surfing the Internet. A rickety old chair from the garage looked strangely out of place as it squatted in front of the keyboard. The oak chair squeaked when anyone sat on it.

"I think your mother is mad at me," Slick said after he caught his breath. "What did you do?"

"I had a little accident this morning," Winky said, hoping that would satisfy Slick's curiosity.

"Did you get hurt?" Slick asked.

"No. I bypassed the stairs today and slid down the banister," Winky explained. "When I reached the bottom, I was going too fast to stop. That's when I broke the vase with the umbrellas stuffed in it."

"Tell your mother what happened," said Slick. "She'll understand that it was an accident."

"I tried, but she didn't want to hear my explanation," Winky said. "I wish I could invent a way to flip a switch and turn into a grownup whenever I wanted. That would be neat."

"Well, once we build this time machine of yours, we'll be all set," Slick said, and then scanned the room, hoping to catch a glimpse of Winky's latest invention.

When his eyes made contact with the door, the doorknob began turning. Slick backed up against the far wall, fearing he had accidentally activated Winky's time machine.

"Look, Winky, the doorknob!" shouted Slick. "You did it! A telepathic time machine." Slick waited for a mysterious creature from the past to enter Winky's room.

The door creaked open, but the entity looked familiar. Winky's dad walked through the time portal carrying a belt.

"Thanks, Winky," Fred whispered while he finished dressing for work. "I always hated that white vase."

"Is there anything else you want Winky to destroy?" Slick asked, and Fred gave him a look. "I was just kidding around Mr. Studmire. You know me."

"I hope so," Fred said as he guided his brown belt through the seven loops on his pants. "I think breaking the vase was enough for today."

"Dad, it was an accident," Winky said before Slick could get him into any more trouble.

"I know that," Fred said. "But if I were you, I'd stay in my room until your mother goes out."

"I'll be hiding in the garage for the rest of the day," Winky said.

"That's a good idea," Fred said. "Have fun, and don't make a mess."

"We will—we're building a time machine. I'll bring you back a souvenir from dinosaur times," Slick said, and Winky's father laughed as he left the room.

"You do that," Fred said. "I could use a good paperweight down at the office."

"Why did you have to say that?" Winky asked once he heard his father tromping down the stairs. "Everyone knows that you can't build a real time machine."

"But I thought that's what we were going to do today," Slick said, confused.

Winky quickly corrected himself. "Oh yeah, the time machine, right." He glanced at a flyer lying on his desk.

Winky had found the perfect weekend project when he spotted the flyer downtown earlier that week. The Mystic Bay Science Association was sponsoring a contest to see who could design the best electric car. There was no minimum age requirement like there was in most competitions. Anyone could enter this contest, even kids in school. He tried to tantalize Slick. "We could disguise our time machine as an electric car and get rich along the way!"

He handed Slick the flyer. Slick read it, but just rolled his eyes.

Clearly, the challenge would be convincing Slick that this was going to be fun. Anything that remotely resembled work was an automatic turnoff for Slick. For Winky, the thousand-dollar grand prize for the electric car competition was plenty motivating.

"Plus, you get to name our design!" said Winky, trying to sweeten the pot.

The precise nature of the vehicle wasn't spelled out. Winky decided that an electric car that looked like a time machine had possibilities, and if calling his entry a time machine was what it took to get Slick to help out, then so be it.

While Winky studied his design sketch, Slick stared out at the bay. He watched the seagulls playing tag as they soared high above the bay. The gulls appeared trapped in time. It was the sea breeze that made them appear motionless, but it was fun to pretend. The birds put him in mind of pictures hanging on a blue wall.

A ladybug made the mistake of landing on Winky's windowpane, just above the grease print left behind by Slick's nose. Slick crushed the bug. Then, he wiped his thumb on his pants. That was a mistake.

"Whew. Did you know that ladybugs stink?" Slick asked after taking a whiff of his thumb.

"Why did you have to do that?" Winky asked. "Now my room is going to smell like squashed bugs."

"I'm bored," Slick yawned.

"Good, because I've got plenty for us to do" Winky said. "Our time machine has to run on electricity; it can't pollute the environment."

"Like we're the experts on harnessing solar energy," Slick said and went back to Winky's window. "Besides, you said that time machines don't exist."

"That's because I haven't bothered to design one. Why do you always give up so easily?" asked Winky. "That's why you get the grades you do. Why won't you even try to win this contest?"

"That's simple; it will take a zillion dollars to build an electric car. That's more than the prize money," Slick said, now more depressed than ever.

"Why would it cost so much?" Winky asked.

"We would need like a thousand batteries to operate an electric car, probably more to power a time machine," Slick pointed out. "Have you seen how much they charge for just a three-pack of 'D' batteries at Dingledorf's?"

"We'll need something more powerful than 'D' batteries for this project. I know where we can get as much power as we need, and it won't cost us a cent," Winky said, stuffing his blueprint in his back pocket. "Let's go to the garage and inventory my dad's junk collection before we do anything else. If we're lucky, we will find most of the parts we need to enter this contest out there."

"I hope you realize that the Mystic Bay Science Association won't let you enter your father's car in their contest," Slick said, but tagged along as Winky tromped down the stairs and barged into the kitchen.

Winky had that determined look in his eyes. Slick had seen that stare before. It always meant that whatever they were going to do, it certainly wouldn't be boring. At least it would be better than watching the seagulls flying out over the bay, or thumb-squashing ladybugs on Winky's windowpane.

"Who said you could come downstairs? You are still in trouble for breaking that vase," said Winky's mother as the boys attempted to sneak behind her in the kitchen.

"Slick wanted to play outside," said Winky.

"Ok," said Winky's mom. "You aren't planning on breaking anything else are you?"

"No, but we are going to take Mr. Studmire's car apart and build an electric car, maybe even a time machine if we have enough parts left over," Slick said before Winky had a chance to answer. "We are going to enter a contest and win lots of money."

"I don't think so," Mrs. Studmire laughed. "Mr. Studmire drove his car to work this morning. And besides, I don't think either of you are old enough to drive a motorized vehicle in Mystic Bay."

"See," Slick said. "That's why we should build the time machine first. With a time machine, we could be sixteen anytime we wanted."

"I'm going out to the garage to play with my wagon. I think that I am old enough to drive it around Mystic Bay," Winky said, and walked out on the back porch before Slick could get him into more trouble. "Come on, Slick, we've got work to do."

"You can't enter a wagon in that contest. I'm going home," Slick said once he was out on the porch.

"I can after I make a few modifications. It will be the fastest electric car in Mystic Bay, if we get lucky with our power source," Winky said. "I'll call it a 'compact car for kids.' How does that sound?"

"Pretty lame if you ask me," Slick said. "Plus, I thought you said I could name it. I'd call it the *Slickster 1000*." Slick paused to let the genius of the name sink into Winky's head. Winky just stared at him. "I guess it doesn't really matter what we call it. Who would be dumb enough to pay us a thousand dollars for a red wagon?"

Winky flinched. "No, no. Hang on, Slick! It won't be a wagon for long."

Slick look intrigued.

"Winky, Slick?" Mrs. Studmire called out from her kitchen window. "Are you boys in the garage?"

"Yes, Mom, I'm out here."

"I put a plate of sandwiches in the refrigerator in case you two get hungry while you are working on your project," Linda said to the boys. "Don't eat anything else in the refrigerator until I come home."

"Okay, Mom," Winky called out from the garage.

Winky forgot all about the sandwiches almost instantly as he began rummaging through the collection of odds and ends his father had acquired over the years. Most of what the boys needed to build the *Slickster 1000* was collecting dust on the shelves. Only the throttle and power source were missing.

"When can we eat those sandwiches?" Slick asked after running back to the kitchen window. "What kind of sandwiches did you make? How many are there?"

"Wait on the porch. I'll put the sandwiches in a paper bag and bring them out to you. I don't want you tracking any dirt from the garage into my kitchen," Linda said and started to close her window before any dust could pollute her clean house.

Slick waited patiently out on the rear steps. His mouth began to water just thinking about food. He loved Mrs. Studmire's sandwiches. They were the best peanut butter and jelly sandwiches in Mystic Bay.

"Here you are," Linda said and handed Slick the bag of sandwiches. "I made a few extra ones just for you. I even trimmed off the crust. Winky told me how much you hate eating bread crust."

"Thanks. Where are you going, Mrs. Studmire?" Slick asked while Winky made some additions to his design sketch.

"I will be down at the Mystic Bay flea market," Linda answered. "Why did you ask?"

"I wanted to say goodbye in case we succeed in building our time machine," Slick said. "Goodbye."

"Goodbye, Slick," Linda laughed and shook her head. "Kids. What an imagination. A time machine!"

"Maybe I will mail you a postcard from the future, Mrs. Studmire," Slick said as an afterthought. "Would you like me to do that?"

"Yes. Take your sandwiches out to the garage and stay out of my kitchen," Linda said, closed the back door, and then headed off for the flea market.

"Winky, look at all the peanut butter sandwiches your mother made us," Slick said. "Do you want one?"

"You can eat them all. I prefer my baloney-smothered-in-mustard sandwiches," Winky said, and went back to studying his wagon's construction.

It was a large, steel wagon built for three, maybe four kids. The wagon had wooden railings on all four sides that made it the perfect tank when they played war. You could see out between the wooden slats and pretend that you were inside a tank, not sitting on it. Football helmets with extension cords tied to them served as their communications headgear.

A tree limb and a branch was their usual weaponry. Sometimes, however, they used Mr. Studmire's umbrella for a gun turret. An empty paper towel roll taped on top of the umbrella made the perfect imaginary cannon. Having an imaginary cannon had its advantages. It never missed its target, and nothing was ever out of range.

"Aren't you hungry?" Slick asked as he unwrapped his first sandwich of the morning. "Now this is a sandwich: fresh bread, tons of peanut butter, and gobs of grape jelly. I love sandwiches with no crusts."

Winky shook his head instead of answering. He was too busy concentrating on his wagon to entertain Slick or get his hands sticky eating jelly sandwiches. The wagon would make the perfect electric car. It was lightweight and maneuverable.

All they needed was a source of power, an electric motor, and a way to control the speed of their car.

The motor wouldn't be a problem, but finding the right power source and throttle might be.

"This is going to be exciting traveling through time," Winky said while he pictured what their electric car would look like when completed. "We'll enter it as the *Slickster 1000*."

"Really? I didn't think you were listening to me. We will be the only kids in Mystic Bay with a time machine. Where are we going to find a battery powerful enough to make it work?" Slick asked as he clicked on the flashlight hanging near the workbench. "The batteries in your dad's flashlight are too weak. They barely make the light bulb glow."

"Those batteries are too small. The ones we need are in the Mystic Bay Sanitary Landfill," Winky said. "I saw Milo Snitzer dump two of his tour bus batteries out there while I was riding my bicycle."

"Why do we need bus batteries?" asked Slick.

"That's the size we'll need to make the *Slickster 1000* operational," Winky explained. "Can you help me find them and bring them back to the garage?"

"Sure, but those batteries are probably dead. Milo wouldn't throw away two good bus batteries," Slick said and took another bite out of his sandwich.

"Milo's batteries might be too weak to start a bus, but I'll bet there is enough power left in them for our time machine," Winky said and had a sudden urge to eat. "Give me one of those sandwiches."

The aroma of peanut butter and grape jelly filled the garage. Winky sat down and unwrapped his sandwich. The boys ate one after another until they were gone. It was a long walk out to the landfill.

Winky knew he would lose his appetite if he waited until they got to the dump before eating. Garbage—ripened by the sun--was the chief ingredient that made up the landfill.

"Let's go," Winky said when he finished eating, and started out of the garage pulling the wagon behind him. "If we hurry, we should be back by suppertime."

"Good. We're having pot roast for supper tonight," Slick said. Slick's world revolved around two events: eating and playing. Anytime that Winky wanted to take Slick's mind off of what was bothering him, he would simply start a conversation that included one or the other. It was a simple formula that always worked.

A loud squeak followed the boys out of the garage. One wheel on the wagon needed oiled and protested noisily as it turned on its axle. Winky was too excited about his project to notice. Slick was too busy gulping down the last of the sandwiches.

Halfway down Cemetery Road, almost a mile from Winky's house, Slick was the first to notice just how bad the squeak was. And the noise appeared to be getting louder with every turn of the wheel.

"I wish we had an oil can with us," Slick said then spit, repeatedly, on the rear axle and wheel.

"Well, we didn't bring one," Winky said while he continued pulling the wagon down the bumpy road.

"Start pushing and stop spitting on the wagon wheels."

"Spit is just as good as oil," Slick said.

Slick tried his best to lubricate the rusty bearings. His slobbering on them didn't do the job. If anything, the bearings were making a louder noise now that they were wet. This did not go unnoticed.

"Why did you have to do that?" Winky asked. "I don't know whether it's you or the squeak that's giving me this headache."

"This is going to be one noisy time machine," Slick observed. "We won't be able to sneak up on the British back in 1776 until we get rid of this squeak."

Winky said nothing. The damage could not be undone. Besides, he was too busy trying to remember exactly where Milo tossed the old bus batteries in the landfill. He had a general idea of where they were located. With a little luck, he would find them and be home in time before it started storming.

Then, a barking ball of fur came racing toward him and interrupted his thoughts.

"Look, Slick, here comes Scooter," Winky said and stooped down to greet the friendly beagle.

Scooter raced past Winky and jumped into the wagon. First, a black nose, and then a pink tongue peeked up over the wooden slat. Sad-looking eyes and two floppy ears quickly followed. Scooter's head was now hanging out over the front of the wagon. The beagle barked out directions that made Winky laugh.

"Why do you talk to Scooter as though you understand what he's saying?" Slick finally asked. "No one can translate dog barks, not even you."

"I know this is going to sound silly, but I know what he's barking," Winky said. "He is a very intelligent beagle."

"Scooter's got smarts?" Slick asked. "I wonder if he could help me with my homework. Does he know how to solve statement problems?"

"I don't think so," Winky admitted.

"Do you think Scooter understands me?" Slick asked, and then eyed the beagle.

"Of course," Winky said. "Try having a conversation with him. But don't try it if there is a cat nearby. Cats interrupt his concentration."

"So you can understand Scooter, big deal," Slick said, and Scooter started barking. "I couldn't make out a single bark. I give up. What did he say?"

"Scooter said that he wants a ride to the landfill," Winky said, and both boys laughed as Scooter barked out orders while sitting in the wagon.

"Tell him about our *Slickster 1000*," Slick said. "Make sure that he knows that it's really going to be our time machine."

"You just did. We've got to oil that wheel when we get back to the garage," Winky said.

"Tell me about it," Slick said. "I'm the one back here by the squeak."

"Scooter says to stop complaining," Winky said.

"He didn't say that," Slick said.

"How do you know?" Winky asked.

"Because he didn't bark," said Slick.

The bickering continued all the way down Cemetery Road. And it didn't stop until the boys reached the path that led to the landfill. At least Winky thought they reached the path. Now, he wasn't so sure.

It wasn't marked, and there was more than one path leading into the woods. Hiking trails were one of the many attractions offered by the town of Mystic Bay for those tourists that preferred looking at the water from a distance.

Slick wasn't concerned. The wagon wasn't moving; the wheel wasn't squeaking; and he took a much-needed break. His back was hurting from pushing both the wagon, and the beagle, down the road.

The hike to the dump stalled. Slick was busy daydreaming of riding his *Slickster 1000* into the past and scaring a few dinosaurs. Winky was wondering if he had chosen the correct path, and Scooter was taking a short nap inside the wagon.

---

Real pictures from the events of this chapter are available at **www.WinkyStudmire.com**. Be sure to comment on your favorite posts, because Winky and Slick always try to respond to their friends!

## CHAPTER 2
### *A Trip to the Dump*

Winky's mom, Linda Studmire, was halfway to the flea market when a low-flying gull caused her to duck. When she looked up to see if the bird was gone, she couldn't help but notice the color of the sky. It was a yellowish-green, with dark clouds hovering out over Mystery Island. A storm was brewing.

"Darn stunt birds!" Verne Randolph yelled as he watched the gull fly upside-down out across the bay. The elderly farmer approached Winky's mom to see if she was okay. "Did that bird attack you?"

"No, Verne, I'm fine," said a shaken Linda.

"Those seagulls keep flying into my Betsy," Verne said and shook his fist at the birds overhead.

"Who's Betsy?" Linda asked.

"My tractor," Verne said.

"Betsy's a nice name for a tractor," Linda said.

"Watch out for those stunt birds," Verne said as he headed off for the pier.

"Thanks for the warning," Linda said, but Verne was already out of earshot.

Linda decided to go back to the house for her umbrella. It would make a good shield against any more stunt bird attacks, and it looked like it was going to rain earlier than predicted. The storms in Mystic Bay could be violent, and the anvil-shaped cloud out over Mystery Island was growing larger by the minute.

As Linda walked home, she kept remembering Slick's promise to mail her a post card from the future. Linda laughed at the thought of Winky and Slick traveling through time.

Two raindrops landing on her forehead startled her back to the present. Linda ran up the street and quickly disappeared inside her house. Automatically reaching out for her umbrella, a handful of air was all she managed to grasp. Then, Linda remembered what happened to her porcelain umbrella vase and walked over to the hall closet.

It took a few seconds to locate her umbrella in all the clutter. She made a mental note to look for another umbrella vase, perhaps an unbreakable brass one, while she was down at the flea market.

Before heading back into town armed with her umbrella, Linda checked her kitchen. Satisfied that Winky and Slick had not confiscated any of her appliances to build their time machine, she left the house for the second time that day, now armed against the weather and low-flying stunt birds.

\*\*\*

"Dive bombers at twelve o'clock," Slick said and hit the dirt. "Winky, get down."

Both Winky and Scooter joined Slick when the seagull bounced off the wooden side rail of their wagon. The dazed gull quickly recovered and flew away. For a brief moment, it was quiet out on Cemetery Road. Then, Slick started complaining again.

"You really should have oiled that wagon wheel before we started out for the landfill," Slick said. "Even the seagulls hate that sound."

Scooter agreed. The squeak was now a higher pitch that hurt his ears more than it did Winky or Slick's. Finally, the beagle registered a complaint with Winky.

"I didn't notice the squeak back in the garage," Winky explained to Scooter. "I'm sorry. I was too busy designing the three-part drive train for our electric car. We're calling it the *Slickster 1000*. I'm entering it in a contest to win a thousand bucks."

"The name was my idea," Slick said to Scooter. "We're really building a time machine."

"It's not polite to interrupt," Winky said. "I was talking to Scooter. He wanted to know all about our entry and the prize money."

"I hope you can make our wagon look like a real time machine," Slick said. "The Mystic Bay Science

Association isn't going to give us that much money for entering a squeaky wagon with two bus batteries tied to it. Your design better work."

Scooter barked that he agreed with Slick. Winky was a little irritated at being criticized by a beagle that was too lazy to walk to the dump.

"Perhaps you would prefer walking to the dump," Winky said. "I decide who rides in my wagon, not Slick. You better be careful how you bark at me."

Scooter thought for a moment, took some time to attack a flea on his hindquarters, and then growled at Slick. He wasn't about to ruin a good thing. A free ride to the dump wasn't something to be ignored.

Winky was trying to remember which trail led to the dump. The dirt path was usually easy to navigate. Today, it wasn't, thanks to a wet spring and fewer tourists than usual. The ground was soft and the weeds were on the rampage.

"Cemetery Road is longer when you have to walk down it," Slick said, resuming his long list of complaints. "We should have brought our bikes. I'm tired of pushing this wagon."

"We had to bring the wagon," Winky said. "How would we transport the batteries on our bicycles?"

"I never thought about that," Slick admitted. "It's a good thing you are in charge of this project."

"I'm not so sure about that," said Winky. "The path to the woods is thick with weeds. We might not make it to the landfill and back before the storm comes ashore."

"We could if we got rid of this wagon," Slick said. "I'll hide it in the weeds. We can pick it up on our way home or come back for it after the storm blows over."

"We can't leave it behind," Winky said. "We need my wagon to carry the parts for our electric car, remember?"

"You mean our time machine," Slick said. "Why do you keep calling it an electric car?"

"Because that's what the Mystic Bay Science Association wants us to build," Winky said, thinking quickly to cover his mistake. "If we call it a time machine, then we can't enter it in the contest. Can't you get that into you head?"

"So even though we're calling it an electric car, it's really a time machine you're designing," Slick said, and waited for confirmation.

"Your *Slickster 1000* is going to be a time machine," Winky said and changed the subject before Slick got wise to his scheme. "This is the shortest way to the dump. We will have to take this path."

The boys managed to push and pull the wagon through the tall grass with some difficulty, but it wasn't as hard as they expected. The only real problem was Scooter. The beagle kept leaping in and out of their wagon now that the boys were busy pushing and pulling it. On one leap, Scooter managed to tip it over.

"That beagle is driving me crazy," Slick said.

"Now, you know exactly how your teacher feels whenever she sees you walking into her classroom," Winky said and then laughed.

Slick didn't think Winky's comment was very funny, and he continued complaining. "Is it just me, or is this path getting steeper with every step?"

They finally crossed the open field and came face-to-face with the dreaded woods.

"This hill is steeper than it looked from the road," Winky said as he studied the path leading through the woods to the Mystic Bay Sanitary Landfill.

"I'm getting tired," Slick said and decided to take a break. "How much further do we have to go before we reach the batteries?"

"Keep pushing and don't think about it." Winky grabbed the wagon handle. "It's going to get a lot easier once we reach the top of this hill."

"Why's that?" Slick asked.

"It will be all *downhill* to the landfill once we clear this grade," Winky said. "The three of us can take a long rest while we coast down to the dump in the wagon. This is going to be a blast."

The wooded hill proved harder to climb than it first appeared, and then there was that ever-annoying squeak. Finally, the boys, their wagon, and the squeak reached the crest of the hill. Scooter was already there.

"Meet the world's laziest dog," Winky said.

The little beagle was snoozing on the trail, curled up on a dry patch of ground. He didn't even twitch a muscle when they approached. His ears remained flopped to one side, and his legs pointed outward.

Winky decided to be kind and steered the wagon around the little beagle. Slick wanted Winky to run over Scooter's tail, but he didn't.

"It sure does smell up here," Winky said. "Put a rock behind the rear wheel before we lose the wagon. I don't want to pull it up that hill a second time."

"Neither do I," Slick agreed, sniffed the air, and almost gagged when he caught a whiff of rotting garbage. "We are definitely heading in the right direction."

Winky surveyed the dump. "I hope we can find the batteries down there."

"I thought you knew where Milo dumped them," Slick said as he put a rock behind the rear wheel of the wagon.

"I do," Winky said. "They're down there in the landfill. I'm not sure exactly where."

"Well that narrows it down, doesn't it?" Slick said. "There has to be miles of garbage down there!"

"Maybe we should consider walking down this hill instead of riding in the wagon," Winky said when he saw that this side of the hill was steeper than the one they had just conquered. "What do you think?"

"Not on your life," Slick said. "I'm tired of walking. And besides, my back hurts from bending over this wagon. You said we could ride all the way down to the landfill once we reached the top of this hill."

"I know, but I'm not so sure now. This hill looks too steep to try in the wagon," Winky said. What was first intended to be a long, relaxing ride to the Mystic Bay Sanitary Landfill now looked more like a suicide mission.

"Come on, Winky; it'll be fun," Slick said and slapped Winky on the back. "Let's pretend that we're in the Mystic Bay Olympics. Instead of a wagon, this is our bobsled, and we're making our final run for the gold."

Against his better judgment, Winky got into the wagon with Slick and Scooter. Winky was squashed up front, followed by Scooter, and then Slick. The side rails on Winky's wagon would make escaping impossible once they started their run down the slope.

"Everybody lean forward as soon as I remove this rock. Rats," Winky said when he realized where he was sitting. "Slick, can you get that rock for me?"

"Sure thing. You just concentrate on steering our bobsled. Remember, this is for the gold medal," Slick said as he easily pushed the rock aside.

"Okay, everyone lean forward," Winky Studmire, captain of the Mystic Bay bobsled team, said to his three-man crew.

Scooter barked, giving Winky more last-minute instructions on the best way to navigate his make-believe bobsled down the killer slope. Winky nodded that he understood the dangers and crossed his fingers for luck.

They were going to need it. Winning the black-and-blue medal was a definite possibility.

Their wagon took off like a shot. It plunged over the edge of the giant hill and began picking up speed at an alarming rate.

"We're all going to die!" Slick yelled when he got his first glimpse of the hill from Winky's vantage point.

"Hold on!" Winky yelled back as he concentrated on getting the three of them and his wagon down the hill without running into a tree.

# CHAPTER 3
## *A Tragic Loss*

"Watch out for that tree!" Slick screamed in Winky's ear.

"I saw it!" Winky struggled to maintain control of their vehicle.

The trail leading to the dump appeared to narrow as the boys' wagon continued gaining speed. Any thoughts of winning the imaginary Mystic Bay bobsled race quickly vanished. Now, just surviving the ride to the bottom became Winky's top priority. His field of vision was reduced to a brown blur with triangular splotches of green racing up the slope, making it appear as if the pine trees were moving as the wagon whizzed past them.

Three bodies--and a single tail held high like a police antenna--bounced back and forth against the wagon's wooden railings. The flimsy slats rattled about, but didn't break. They held both boys captive.

Going down this side of the hill was more like riding on a roller coaster that had suddenly decided to abandon its tracks. Their wagon was plummeting out of control on a collision course with the dump.

The possibility that they might swerve off the path into one of the many pine trees was high. Winky fought hard to keep the wagon on course. Their *Slickster 1000* wasn't designed to race over bumps at high speeds. Each rut tossed the front wheels off the ground, making steering impossible until the front wheels once again made contact with the path. The few seconds that their front wheels were airborne seemed more like hours to Winky.

Slick could do nothing except watch and scream. He was trapped in the rear of the wagon surrounded on three sides by wooden side rails. After hitting several ruts in rapid succession, only Slick's head was visible above the slats. He was playing it safe and ducked down as far as possible.

Scooter was partially wedged under Slick's legs. His antenna-like tail and rear-end were still exposed and pointing skyward. Convinced that he was safe, Scooter whapped Winky in the head with his tail.

"This *is* a time machine!" Slick shouted when the wagon shot out over another cliff halfway down the hillside. "I'll bet we're halfway to tomorrow!"

Winky would have laughed had he not been so busy concentrating on avoiding the trees that lined both sides of the trail. Once the front wheels touched down and gripped the dirt, Winky made an immediate course correction. They would be safe for a few more seconds at least.

Winky began to relax when the path started to smooth out. The wagon's handle was no longer trying to rip itself free of his hands.

Steering the wagon became easier. The deep ruts and hard bumps were behind them. It looked like they were going to make it down the hill without wrecking.

Nothing could have been further from the truth.

Suddenly, all four wheels were barely touching the path. "Our wagon is gaining speed!" Winky shouted.

A terrified Scooter leaped out of the wagon while there was still time to escape.

A handful of fleas abandoned the beagle just before he jumped ship. Three of the fleas were now quietly grazing on Winky's back. Ten more fleas were preparing to dine on Slick's right leg. For the fleas, the move turned out to be a gourmet's delight. Both boys were delicious.

All itching was placed on hold until later. There was a bigger problem dead ahead. And it was racing toward them, or vice versa. Winky would need a miracle to get around this obstacle and still remain on the path. A quick glance told him there was no way out.

It looked like their ride to the dump was over.

"We're going to hit whatever that is," Winky said. "Brace yourself and try to protect your head."

"Ten-four," Slick said to let Winky know that he heard the warning, and then ducked down until his head finally drooped below the wooden side railings.

Accepting his fate and chalking it up to bad judgment on his part, Winky stared out at the huge bump in the trail ahead. Neither boy said another word. There was nothing to do but hope that the wagon's axles would survive the impact. The wagon was going too fast to risk any type of evasive maneuver.

Now, even the slightest turn of the wheels might cause the wagon to flip at this speed. Winky knew that his best chance of walking away from this smashup was to hit the bump straight on. He crossed his fingers for good luck. This collision looked like it was going to be brutal.

Both boys screamed when their wagon made contact with an exposed tree root. Fortunately, mud from previous rains had settled on the upper side of the massive root and had turned it into a giant inclined plane.

Instead of smashing directly into the root and coming to a catastrophic end, their wagon simply zoomed up the ramp and kept on going. It seemed to have a mind of its own as it chose to abandon the path littered with ruts, tree roots, and ramps. The wagon set a new course for the clouds coming in off the bay.

Surprisingly, neither boy panicked while the wagon continued skyward. After the initial jolt that shot them upward, the ride proved to be exciting, and surprisingly smooth. It was a welcome change from the bumpy trail below. There was no sensation of speed, and no squeaking wheel to annoy them. It was almost too quiet.

But that was all about to change.

Instead of dreamy white clouds, the dump came into view as their wagon continued on its arc back to earth. Slick's time machine was about to crash, and the landing was going to be ugly. A fresh load of garbage was waiting to break their fall.

"Hold your breath!" Winky yelled as the wagon locked onto a fresh pile of garbage like a cruise missile homing in on its target.

A wet, sticky sound filled their ears as the wagon buried itself deep in the trash. The sound reminded Winky of tromping through gooey mud in his tennis shoes. The feeling was wet and cold, but they were safe. Both boys fought their way to the surface.

"Whew, that was some landing. I never thought that we would walk away from that trip in one piece," Slick said. He held his nose and started wading toward land that was covered by grass instead of refuse.

Winky began wiping off the gobs of used coffee grinds, rotten banana peels, and moldy green bread that were now clinging to his clothes, face, and arms.

Slick had chocolate pudding on one of his hands and was almost tempted to sample it. His shirt was covered with brown rice and a sticky orange sauce. A smelly juice that looked like water--but smelled like garbage--soaked the cuffs of his pants and shoes.

Scooter had finished his trip down the hill on foot, and greeted the boys near the edge of the landfill. He wanted to play fetch-the-stick. The beagle trotted up to the boys, dropped a branch that he found, and suddenly stepped back. One whiff and Scooter quickly decided to keep his distance.

"Let's wash off this garbage before we do anything else," Winky said. "I don't know about you, but I can't stand having this goop on me."

"Okay, where's the water spigot?" Slick asked.

"Hazard Creek," Winky said and noticed that Slick was reluctant to go. "We'll avoid the rapids and rinse off in the shallows. As soon as our clothes are clean, we'll start searching for Milo's batteries."

Slick smiled when Winky mentioned the shallows. As long as they avoided the rapids, he was happy. Once in the water, the boys stripped down to their boxer shorts and washed themselves thoroughly.

Next, Winky and Slick washed their clothes as best they could in the creek, considering they didn't have any soap. Slick was careful to rinse out all of his pockets. He didn't want to reach into one of them later on and find any surprises waiting for him.

"I hate wearing wet clothes," said Winky.

"Tough beans. Let's start looking for those batteries," Slick said. "I came out here to find parts for the *Slickster 1000*."

Winky was surprised by Slick's enthusiasm. "You're absolutely correct," said Winky. The boys headed back to the dump.

It was a short walk from Hazard Creek to the Mystic Bay Sanitary Landfill. Directions were not needed; all you had to do was follow your nose. Once they reached the landfill, Winky and Slick immediately began scanning the outer edges of the dumpsite for Milo's old bus batteries.

Nothing looked familiar to Winky. He had left a long trail of restaurant pickle jars behind during his last visit as markers where the batteries were buried. It seemed like a logical choice at the time. The huge jars were made out of heavy plastic and stood out from the rusty tin cans. They also reflected the sunlight.

The jars were all now just a few inches beneath the surface and totally useless, buried in a sea of trash.

"I can't remember where they are," Winky finally said. "I thought the batteries were over here. I marked the spot with jars, but they all seem to have disappeared. Are you having any luck?"

"Not yet," Slick said, as he examined a rusty tricycle with two wheels.

"Well, keep searching. Maybe we'll get lucky."

Scooter barked off in the distance. He was trying to capture Winky's attention. Seeing that he wasn't having any success, the beagle decided to sit and watch. Sooner or later, Winky would come to him.

"Slick, be careful where you walk," Winky said to his pal. "Some of this garbage acts like it's floating on water. Look how spongy it is."

The dumpsite was not static like a backyard. It constantly changed its appearance with every new load of garbage. The odds of returning to the exact same spot in the dump without a marker would be slim at best.

"Winky, look!" Slick said, pointing out to the spot where they had crashed into the dump.

"Did you find the batteries?" Winky asked, and turned to see what was holding Slick's attention. "Oh, no."

"This can't be happening to us," Slick said. "First, your pickle jars disappear, and now, this."

Winky and Slick sat down on the grass and watched the *Slickster 1000* slowly sink out of sight. Both boys realized it was too dangerous to risk wading back into the new landfill area to rescue it. Even the wooden side rails had sunk in the watery goop. The wagon's handle was all that was visible.

The handle resembled a periscope on a submarine. It remained a good six inches above the garbage as though it were searching for a victim to torpedo. Then, it too slowly sank beneath the waves of refuse.

"There goes our time machine, lost forever under an ocean of garbage," Winky said and couldn't hide his disappointment. "I really thought we had a good chance of winning that first prize money."

"That's okay; it could have been worse," Slick was quick to point out to Winky. "Imagine one of us sinking out there instead of your wagon."

"You're right about that. We were lucky this time. It's a good thing we ran for solid ground as soon as we crashed," Winky said. "I hate to think how deep that pool of garbage might be over there."

"What are we going to do now? Go home?" Slick asked. "The wagon is gone, and so is our chance of winning the thousand dollars."

"I'm not ready to give up on winning that prize money. We will just have to find everything we need to build our time machine out here in the landfill. There has to be another wagon out here, somewhere," Winky said, and then looked over at his pal only to see something squirming on his pants. "Worms! Slick, you must have sat on some worms."

"So did you, so there," Slick said. "How are we going to get them off of our pants?"

"Hazard Creek," Winky answered and started running toward the creek with Slick chasing after him.

The boys raced back to the creek and dove into the water. It didn't seem so cold now that they were trying to wash off the worms from the dump. Both Winky and Slick stripped down again to make sure that no worms were clinging to their skin. Only when they were positive that they were worm-free did they begin rinsing off their clothing that was floating in the water.

The trout in Hazard Creek received an unexpected treat for lunch--fresh worms from the Mystic Bay Sanitary Landfill, courtesy of Winky and Slick.

Overhead the clouds grew darker and darker, and thunder began to rumble.

# CHAPTER 4
## *A Change in Plans*

"I don't want to go back to the landfill," Slick said while pinching his nose to keep out the creek water. "The only thing I ever find there is worms and soggy garbage. Plus, the dump ate my *Slickster 1000*. I might be next on the menu!"

"So stay here and swim with all the little worms floating downstream," Winky said. "I thought you wanted to win the contest, but that's okay. Scooter and I will be happy to split the thousand dollars."

"We've already lost our time machine's body. What good are the batteries without the frame and wheels?" Slick asked. "We'll never find another wagon out here in all this garbage, at least one in good condition. I think it's time to go home."

"I hate going home empty-handed," Winky said.

Though Winky didn't want to admit it, Slick was making sense. Without their wagon, building an electric car for kids would be impossible. The boys would never be able to meet the deadline for the entries if they had to start from scratch.

Then, a sound off in the distance caught their attention.

"Listen, do you hear that?" Winky asked.

"I'd recognize that squeak anywhere," Slick said. "It's the *Slickster 1000*! Scooter must have rescued it from the dump, but how?"

"I think you might be right," Winky said as he spotted Scooter pulling something towards them. "No, it's too small to be my wagon," he said, and raced up the bank to greet the little beagle.

Scooter carefully approached the boys with a small baby wagon. After taking several whiffs and not detecting any garbage smells, he eagerly licked Winky's face.

Both Winky and Slick studied their new wagon from every possible angle. It was tiny compared to Winky's wagon, and very rusty, but it was all they had. Frustrated, Winky turned toward Slick and gave him the bad news.

"This wagon will never be a *Slickster 1000*."

"And why not?" Slick asked. "It has four working wheels and a frame."

"It's too small to hold my original design," Winky said. "What do you think, Scooter? Is it big enough to enter in the contest?"

Scooter barked his answer, and Winky found himself agreeing with him. At times, the little beagle could be very persuasive. Scooter was convinced that anything was possible. And he let Winky know that he expected him to use the wagon instead of giving up.

"I know that it's better than nothing, but it's half the size of our *Slickster 1000*," Winky argued with the beagle. "Where am I going to put the second battery, the power train, and the throttle controls?"

"You don't even have the first battery, so who cares?" Slick said, interrupting their dialog.

Both Winky and Scooter gave Slick a dirty look. His comments weren't welcome at this time. In this case, three heads were not better than two. Slick kept quiet, took a seat on one of the rocks, and quietly observed the pair. He listened first to Winky, and then to Scooter's response. Winky's words made sense to him, but Scooter's barking remained a cleverly-coded message that he was unable to decipher.

"I suppose we could use your wagon for our entry," Winky said after giving the rusty wagon a closer examination. "I'd have to make a few modifications on my original design, but it just might work. You didn't happen to run across Milo's bus batteries while you were out there searching through the landfill, did you? We can't enter the contest without them."

Scooter barked an answer and eagerly awaited an enthusiastic response.

"Really? That's great! Take us to them," Winky said, and Scooter scampered off on his way to the landfill. "Hey, Scooter, come back here. You know we can't keep up with you."

"You've trained him well," Slick said when Scooter ignored Winky's command and disappeared into a wooded area on his way back to the landfill.

"I guess we will have to wait for Scooter to find us, just like he did with the wagon," Winky said.

Slick stared at their new wagon and tried to figure out where he was going to sit. "This wagon is too small, Winky."

The wagon Scooter drudged up from the landfill was barely two-feet wide and not more than four feet long. Its wheels were six inches in diameter, tops, and all four of them squeaked. The new wagon's handle was slightly bent, but so was the one on Winky's wagon. Mystic Bay's hills were hard on wagon handles.

Slick calculated that two of Milo's batteries would devour at least three feet of space. The boys also needed room for the throttle and engine. That would eat up at another foot of interior space on their wagon. You didn't have to be a genius in math to see that they had a problem on their hands.

"I liked your wagon better," Slick said when he saw that using the new wagon was a hopeless exercise.

"So did I, but this is all we have to work with, so get used to it," Winky said. "Keep an eye out for Scooter. I know he wouldn't go home without us. He's probably looking for me."

On cue, Scooter called to the boys from the far side of the landfill. Unable to retrieve Milo's two bus batteries like he had done with the baby wagon, Scooter barked for the boys to come and help him.

The boys gave him a confused look, so Scooter froze in position with his nose pointing toward one of the bus batteries. He raised one paw and pointed his tail skyward for added effect.

"Good boy, Scooter!" Winky said, and motioned for Slick to bring the wagon out into the landfill. "Scooter found Milo's batteries! Come on, it's safe to walk on this garbage. Those heavy bus batteries didn't even put a dent in this stuff."

Slick slowly pulled the rusty wagon over to where Scooter was pointing. All four wheels on the wagon screamed as though they were in pain.

Winky took measurements of the wagon and the batteries using his forearm for a measuring stick. He did this several times in order to double check his calculations. He wasn't satisfied with the results.

"Rats," Winky finally said and plopped down on the wagon. "These measurements mess up everything."

"The wagon's too small, isn't it?" Slick asked.

"How did you know that?" Winky asked.

"I've got eyes," Slick said. "You don't have to be in the gifted class to see that both of those batteries aren't going to fit in this tiny wagon."

Winky made a decision. "We will only use one of Milo's batteries in this wagon," he said, though he was clearly disappointed. "It will definitely limit the range of our entry, but it can't be helped."

"One bus battery will have more than enough power to push this tiny wagon along," Slick said, trying to encourage his pal.

The sky suddenly darkened, causing both boys to glance up at the clouds.

Winky didn't like what he was seeing. "It looks like that big storm they were calling for is headed our way quick."

Scooter began barking hysterically as the clouds overhead rumbled.

"Yeah, it looks like the Genie is getting ready to shoot some lightning bolts at us," Slick said.

"Genie?"

"You know, the Mystic Bay Genie who's mad about being trapped in his lamp and causes all the lightning storms around here," Slick said, matter-of-factly.

"Slick, no wonder you're failing Science." Winky took out his phone to snap a picture of the impressive storm clouds. "It's definitely time to get out of here. Help me load this battery into the wagon."

Now they were beginning to make some progress. Maybe they would get their entry built in time. It would be a tiny compact model, one just for kids--and perhaps a beagle.

"We better hurry. The wind is picking up, and I can hear the thunder off in the distance," Winky said.

Suddenly, a giant lightning bolt flashed across the clouds.

Winky jumped. "Now, *that's* the kind of power source we need to power our entry."

"If we stand here much longer, the Genie's going to grant you your wish," Slick said. "Run for the garage! I don't want to end up looking like a piece of burnt toast." Flashes of light danced across the sky.

The boys took a different route home. It was flatter than the trail they used to get to the landfill, and much safer. The hills around Mystic Bay were a good thing to avoid during a thunderstorm.

---

You can check out Winky's picture from the dump at **www.WinkyStudmire.com**. Be sure to tell Slick what you think about his Genie theory!

# CHAPTER 5
*The Building Begins*

When the wind started tossing the occasional garbage can lid their way, the boys broke into a slow trot. That proved costly. The boys left critical parts for their electric car littering Cemetery Road.

In their haste to get out of the storm, Winky and Slick managed to lose two handfuls of wire, plus a rusty light-dimmer switch they happened to find on their way out of the landfill. The switch was going to be the throttle on their entry and would control the amount of electricity going to the motor.

Only Milo's battery refused to fall out of the wagon. Now that he was back in his garage, Winky was disappointed that he lost the wire and dimmer switch. Slick could have cared less. Scooter wanted to play.

"Not now, Scooter," Winky said to the beagle tugging on his pants. "I have to work on my entry. I want to win those thousand dollars."

"What are we going to use for an engine to propel us through time?" Slick asked after studying the wagon for several minutes. "We are definitely going to need a powerful propulsion unit."

"We are going to use that old attic fan to power our wagon, but we still need to find something that will enable us to control its speed," Winky said. "We will have to slow down on some of the curves. I was really counting on that dimmer switch to do the job."

"That makes sense. I wouldn't want to go too far into the future, or the past. We could always borrow my dad's transformer--you know, the one that controls the trains in his miniature replica of Mystic Bay," Slick said. "I didn't know there were curves in time, Winky."

"Are you sure your dad will allow us to borrow his transformer?" Winky asked, carefully evading Slick's question about time curves. "It's the most expensive transformer down at the Mystic Bay Hobby Shop & Worm Farm. I like that it has dual controls, but your dad will never let us borrow it, not in a million years."

"Of course he will. We just won't ask him. I'm telling you, he'll never know that it's missing," Slick said. "My dad hasn't played with his trains since he found a dead mouse on one of his railroad crossings."

"Why was there mouse on the tracks?" Winky asked.

"I might have put it there so I could play with his trains," Slick said. "My dad's afraid of mice."

"That's perfect!" Winky said. "Once we get the transformer over here, I think we will have everything we need to build our entry and win the prize money."

"What about the wire we lost?" Slick asked.

"Rats, I knew that I was forgetting something," Winky said. "I've looked everywhere in the garage and all I could find were two coat hangers."

"Coat hangers should do the job," said Slick.

"No, we need insulated wire so we don't get shocked," Winky said. "I think we might have to make another trip out to the dump to get more wire."

"I've got a better idea," Slick said, but he wouldn't tell Winky his plan. He started out of the garage with Winky following *him* for a change.

The boys headed off to Slick's house with the empty wagon in tow. It was a lot easier pulling it now that Milo's battery was resting in Winky's garage, but the wagon still squeaked. Off on the horizon, a second storm was building, one with even blacker clouds. You could see the rain bands out on the bay, and it was only a matter of time before it attacked the town.

Once the boys reached Slick's house, Slick sneaked inside to make sure his parents were at work.

Once the coast was clear, the boys went down in the basement to check out the control panel for their entry.

"This will definitely do," Winky said while Slick removed the last wire connecting his father's transformer to the train board.

"I like the dual controls." Slick carefully pushed one lever forward and pulled back on the other. "With two controls, we won't ever have to take turns steering our time machine."

"Okay, where are you going to get the wire we need?" Winky asked. "We're going to need a lot."

"Are you kidding? Take a look under the train board. There must be a million miles of wire down here," Slick said. "What color do you think we'll need, red or black? I've got both."

"You better grab some of each," Winky said, "just to play it safe. "You can never have enough wire on a job like this."

Yards of wire came flying out from beneath the train board. Slick was somewhere under the train set tearing out all of the red and black wire he could reach. Winky began to panic when he noticed how much wire Slick had already removed.

"You better stop ripping out all that wire," Winky said to his pal when a miniature railroad sign toppled onto the tracks. "You knocked over a signal."

"Did you say we need more wire?" asked Slick.

"No, I think we have enough."

Slick's head surfaced. "There's more wire under there. You said that we could never have too much wire."

Winky was struggling with the giant mass of wires they had accumulated, trying to separate the red ones from the black ones. "I was wrong," he said. "We better head back to the garage before that other storm hits. Let's get out of here."

"Gee, I didn't realize that I grabbed so much wire," Slick said after he crawled out from beneath the train board. "I think we better go over to your place before my dad comes home and catches us."

He eyed the top of his father's train set and gave a sigh of relief. "It still looks the same. My dad will never suspect that we were here. I'll carry the transformer; you're in charge of the wire."

It was a short distance to Winky's place, but the weight of the transformer made the walk seem like forever to Slick. His hands ached. It never dawned on either boy to place the transformer on top of the wires in the wagon. Slick ran the last few yards to the garage. He was looking for a place to set the transformer down before his fingers fell off.

"Be careful where you put that transformer," Winky said and carelessly dumped the red and black wires onto the garage floor. "I don't want it to get wet. Sometimes the roof leaks when it rains real hard. Little puddles form where you are standing."

"So where do you want this transformer?" Slick asked. "I can't hold onto it much longer."

"Put it on the workbench," Winky said, and then continued giving out instructions. "Help me mount the attic fan on the back of the wagon. It's heavier than it looks."

"This still doesn't look like a time machine to me," Slick said as he picked up his end of the attic fan.

"Just hold it in place while I clamp it to the wagon." Winky took two large C-clamps off of his dad's workbench.

Slick struggled to hold the heavy fan in place while Winky clamped it to the wagon. With each turn of the clamp, the garage seemed to grow darker.

Then, it began to pour outside.

Winky examined the engine mounts on their entry. "I think these clamps will hold. You can let go now."

The moment Slick released his grip on the fan, the wagon flipped backwards. The wagon was pointing straight up in the air like a rocket ship on its launch pad. Winky's attic fan was too heavy for the smaller wagon. It was the first of many setbacks.

"I told you this wasn't going to work," Slick said. "We need a rocket engine. They are lighter and more powerful than attic fans."

"Did you see any rockets while we were out at the dump?" Winky asked while he studied their dilemma.

"No, but look at this. I think we are going to have trouble steering our time machine, Mr.

Engineer," Slick said and spun the front wheels to amuse himself.

"It's only a minor glitch," Winky said. "I know that I am forgetting something. Give me a minute to go over my design. The wagon should not have flipped like that."

"No kidding," Slick said and stared out at the black clouds that continued rolling in off of the bay.

"I've got it," Winky said. "Slick, help me pull the front wheels down until they touch the concrete."

Once all four wheels were touching the concrete, Winky motioned for Slick to let go while he held the front of the wagon down. This time, the wagon did not flip. Winky needed a counterbalance to keep the front of the wagon from flipping back up in the air.

"Are you going to hold it down like that all day?" Slick asked.

"No, bring your dad's transformer over here and put it in the front of the wagon," Winky said. "Let's see if the transformer is heavy enough to keep the front wheels down on the concrete."

Slick grabbed the transformer off of the workbench and placed it in the front of the wagon. Winky gradually lightened his grip that was holding the wagon in place.

The front wheels started to lift off of the ground just a bit.

"Rats, it's still too light up front," Winky said. "Bring Milo's bus battery over here."

"Where do you want the battery?" Slick asked.

"There's only one place left," Winky said. "Put it in the middle."

Slick squeezed the battery in between the fan and the transformer. The wagon was now full. The front wheels made contact with the concrete and stayed there. The weight problem involving the fan had been solved.

"We finally did it," Winky said and smiled.

"We still have one little problem," Slick pointed out. "Could you show me where we are going to sit?"

"Rats," Winky said again, and went back to his blueprint to correct the latest flaw in his design. "There has to be a way to make this work." He stepped back and snapped a picture of their entry with his phone. "Slick, do you have any ideas?"

"Nope," Slick said, and then turned to watch the lightning bolts flashing from cloud to cloud.

The flashes were getting closer. The thunder was getting louder. Wind was blowing shingles off of the roofs. And the streetlights in Mystic Bay had come on in the middle of the afternoon.

That was a bad sign.

---

To see Winky's photo of his electric car entry, check out his post on April 27, 2013 at **www.WinkyStudmire.com**. He would love to hear what you think of this design!

# CHAPTER 6
## *The Genie's Wrath*

Their electric car was beginning to take shape. Soon, the wagon that served as their chassis would be all but invisible. From the rear, all you could see was a large fan. The top of the wagon was under an oversized battery and a train transformer with dual controls. Red and black wires would hide the sides.

Still, there was something missing.

"We have a little problem, a minor detail that I somehow overlooked," Winky said. "What we need is something to protect us from the fan's blades."

"Why do we need protection from an attic fan?" Slick asked. "It looks harmless enough."

"That's because the fan isn't connected to the battery," Winky said and gave the blades a spin to prove his point. "You have to find something that will prevent us from leaning back into the spinning blades," Winky said. "That's your assignment for today."

"You know how much I hate doing homework," Slick said. "Why don't you go look for it?"

"Because I haven't been able to come up with a solution," Winky said. "Maybe you can figure out how to make the fan safe on our wagon. Will you give it a try? I think you can do it."

"I'll do it if you will tell everyone at school that our entry in the contest is a time machine," Slick said and the negotiating began.

"If that's what it takes to get you to solve this problem, I agree to tell everyone that our entry is an official Mystic Bay time machine," Winky said.

"Okay, where do I begin?" Slick asked.

"Look up in the storage area," Winky said. "I think there's an old rabbit pen up there."

Slick smiled and accepted the challenge. While Winky started attaching wires from the battery to the transformer, Slick climbed a rickety set of stairs that led to a large storage area above the garage. The place was a time machine warehouse.

"Look at all the old junk up here!"

"Just be careful where you step," Winky said to his pal. "None of those floorboards up there are nailed down."

"Don't worry about me; I know what I am doing." Slick started making his way over to an old rabbit pen that had been carefully dismantled by Winky's father. "I think I found it."

"Bring it down here and let me see," Winky said.

"This might take a few minutes," said Slick.

"Okay," Winky said and went back to his wiring.

Slick decided the pen's wire mesh had possibilities. Up close, anyone could see that the wire was heavier than any wire used on a window screen. It would make the perfect shield for the attic fan. Now, Slick had to figure out how to get the mesh down.

"How are you doing up there?" Winky asked.

"I think this is going to work," Slick called down to his pal. "I found some wire mesh up here."

"Well, bring it down here," Winky said, and then started back over to Slick's time machine carrying two armfuls of black wire.

Suddenly, Slick screamed as both he and what he believed to be the solution to their fan problem dropped down from the second floor. He had stepped on the wrong end of a loose board and it flipped—and so did three other boards. A corner of the rabbit pen Slick was carrying caught on a nail sticking out from one of the wooden joists.

The frame stopped abruptly, but Slick and the heavy wire mesh continued downward. Afraid that he might land headfirst on the concrete if he let go, Slick held onto the heavy wire as it tore free from the wooden frame. Slick's head never hit the floor.

"Stop goofing around up there," Winky said when he saw Slick swinging from the joists like a chimpanzee. His fall ended abruptly with his feet dangling only inches above the concrete.

When Slick finally dared to open his eyes, he was pleasantly surprised. He was still alive, and quickly dropped to the floor as though nothing had happened. Next, he pulled the wire mesh free from the nail on the beam above his head. The frame followed—as well as two more loose boards, all narrowly missing both boys. "That was a dangerous maneuver," Winky said and looked up to see if anything else was about to fall from the second floor.

"I tripped on a board," Slick said, "But I think I found a solution to our problem. We can use this heavy wire to protect ourselves from the blades. It looks strong enough to form a protective cage around the fan. What do you think, Winky? Did I do a good job?"

"It's perfect," Winky said, and quickly finished attaching a wire before he forgot where it went.

"I've got to sit down," Slick said. "I'm dizzy."

Their time machine was growing a long moustache of red and black train wires. It looked more like a wagonload of junk than something you would enter in a contest. Now, the boys needed an outer shell to conceal the wires, battery, and the transformer in order to have a chance of winning.

"Wake me when you are finished." Slick yawned. He was battered and bruised from his fall through the joists. Tired, his head began to droop. Sitting gradually turned into a slump forward as he fought to remain awake. It was a losing battle.

As he sat there watching Winky attach the wires to their time machine, his eyes ever so slowly collapsed. Slick knew that he should be helping, but just thinking about standing exhausted him. His legs refused to budge. So, he took a well-deserved nap.

It was still pouring outside. The storm that roared in off the Atlantic had now stalled directly over the town of Mystic Bay. Huge raindrops beating on the garage's roof had a soothing effect on Slick. The droplets lulled him to sleep. Soon he was snoring away, an empty tin can vibrating with every snort.

Winky didn't mind. He was too busy checking the wiring on their time machine to entertain his pal. Time slipped away as he worked. It was still raining.

"Finally, I finished all of the wiring," Winky announced, but Slick continued snoring while sitting on an inverted bucket near the open garage door.

A few drops of rain landed on Slick's shoe. Winky smiled and went back to work making slight adjustments here and there on their entry. Slick never moved from his spot, even when the thunder shook the garage and rattled the windowpanes.

"Slick, wake up," Winky said, hoping to rouse his pal. "This is going to be great! Did you ever see a time machine like this one? Look, your screen idea will protect us from the fan's rotating blades."

"How does it work?" Slick asked, still unsure as to what kind of contraption Winky had designed.

"It's easy to operate," Winky said and looked to see if Slick was paying attention. "All you do is push or pull the dual controls on your dad's train transformer to make the wagon go forward or backward."

"You mean move forward or backward *in time*, don't you?" Slick asked and reminded Winky of their deal. "You promised to call our entry a time machine."

"Whatever. Anyway, if you pull back on the left control, the time machine goes backwards--I mean into the past--and pushing the right control forward makes it go into the future, I think," Winky said. "It could be vice versa; we won't really know until we give it a trial run. We can't do anything outside until this storm moves further up the coast."

"Why not?" Slick asked. "Let's try it out."

"We can't. It's too dangerous to play out in a thunderstorm," Winky said. "I don't want to get zapped. Let's check and see if I forgot anything."

Slick had other plans. The possibility of traveling back in time excited him. And he knew exactly where his first stop would be.

"Do you think I could change some of my old report cards?" Slick asked, clearly impressed by the maze of red and black wire that now enveloped their wagon.

"No. That would be cheating," Winky pointed out.

"I was only kidding," Slick said.

"Let's see. All the wires are properly attached and tightened down. Our engine is in the back, power supply in the middle, and the controls are up front. Tell me, what do you think of my masterpiece?" Winky asked, and waited for Slick's stamp of approval.

"I only have one question," Slick said.

"So ask it," Winky said.

"Where are the seats in this time machine?"

"I knew I was forgetting something," said Winky as he looked around the garage for a way to solve the seating problem on their entry. "Slick, hand me that wooden board over in the corner. This might work."

Winky took the board from Slick and placed it on top of both the battery and the transformer. "This should do the job."

"How are you going to keep that board from falling off of our time machine?" Slick asked.

"With tape--lots of black, plastic tape," Winky said, and he began to use up roll after roll of his father's electrical tape. "Now, we have a cushioned seat, and it's not going to fall off."

Slick helped Winky tape the board on top of the transformer and Milo's battery. Once that was done, Slick continued taping every part of the wagon that had even a hint of rust on its surface. When he was finished, only two control levers peeked out from the layers of tape that wrapped around the wagon. Their contest entry was now complete.

"I think we've run out of plastic tape," Slick said as he rummaged through the many drawers filled with nuts, bolts, and screws in Winky's garage.

"We don't need anymore. I think you mummified our wagon," Winky said. "It's all but invisible."

"I can't believe it; our rusty wagon looks so streamlined," Slick said. "With the wagon taped, you can't tell that it came from the landfill. I think I prefer this compact model now that it is covered with four layers of black plastic."

"Me, too," Winky said as he admired his design.

A yelping Scooter interrupted the boys' discussion. The beagle raced into the garage to get out of the rain.

The storm showed no sign of letting up. If anything, it was getting more violent. Winky pulled out his phone just in time to snap a picture of a gigantic bolt of lightning.

"I've never seen the Genie so angry," Slick said as the thunder boomed outside the garage.

"Will you cool it with the Genie nonsense?" Winky said as he stood back to study his design.

"It's not nonsense! Check out this website that explains all about it." Slick shoved his phone in Winky's face.

His pal chuckled. "I made that page just now to mess with you while you were snoozing on the job.

Come, on; I want to test drive our time machine in the garage."

"You remembered to call it a time machine," Slick said, happy to move beyond the great Genie debate. He watched Winky manipulate the two controls on the transformer, but nothing budged. "Um, when is our entry going to start moving? Isn't the fan supposed to be turning?"

Scooter barked, confirming the fact that Winky had not moved an inch. Winky gave the beagle a nasty look that immediately quieted him down.

"I don't know what's wrong," Winky said. "The fan should be spinning. I know that I wired everything properly."

"I don't think it matters how you wired it," Slick said. "Our time machine won't ever work."

"What makes you think that?" Winky asked. He pushed both levers on the train transformer forward as far as possible. Still, the fan blades did not move.

"Because Milo's battery is dead, that's why. You know Milo; he would never throw a good battery away," Slick said. "If the battery is dead, so is our entry."

"I was convinced that there would be enough juice left in it to power our wagon, but maybe you're right," Winky said. "We should have charged Milo's battery before we sealed it under all that tape. I admit it: I screwed up."

"How are you planning on charging the battery now that it is encased inside our time machine?" Slick asked. "I don't see any exposed terminals."

"You will have to help me peel all of that tape off," Winky said.

"There must be at least a mile of tape wrapped around our wagon!"

"So? You put it on; how hard can it be to peel off? If we're careful, we might be able to use the same tape to seal the battery once it is fully charged." Winky turned to Slick. "What do you think?"

"The contest will be over by the time we get all that tape off," Slick said. "I say forget the whole thing."

"All it needs is a good charge," Winky said. "Let's give it one last try before we give up."

"Okay, but push the wagon out in the rain," Slick said. "Water always loosens tape. It will be easier to unwrap once it is wet."

"I'm not sure we'll be able to reuse the tape once it gets wet," Winky said, but he decided to pull the wagon out of the garage anyway, with Slick pushing from behind. They parked it under the giant oak in his backyard. "Quick, get back in the garage!" Winky yelled once their electric car was in position.

"Once they were back inside the garage, Slick asked, "Why did you park it there? The wagon is supposed to be out in the open, not hidden under a tree. That tape is never going to loosen up under there."

"Why not?" Winky asked. "The wagon's outside in the rain, just like you said."

"There are hardly any raindrops landing on our wagon. Those oak big leaves are acting like tiny umbrellas," Slick pointed out. "Look, most of the dirt around the base of that tree is still dry."

"Why didn't you say something when I put it there?" Winky asked. "I would have moved it!"

"Who had time to look up? I was busy pushing the wagon. You were supposed to be doing the steering," Slick said.

"I'll guess I'll have to go back out and try to move the wagon over to an open area," Winky said and started out of the garage.

Suddenly, there was a flash of light, quickly followed by a loud thunderclap. The rush of hot air entering the garage blew out two windows and knocked both boys off their feet.

---

You can find Winky's photo of the lightning storm—plus a link to a website he created to have a little fun with Slick--at **www.WinkyStudmire.com**. Winky and Slick would love to hear your own ideas about the legend of the Mystic Bay Genie!

# CHAPTER 7
## *Trial Run*


"What was that?" Slick asked as he struggled to his feet.

A dazed Winky was dusting off his trousers. "I think that was a lightning bolt that struck too close to the garage," he said.

"Are you sure it was lightning?" Slick asked. "Did you hear the explosion?"

"I didn't hear a thing," Winky said, "did you?"

"Yes," Slick answered. "I thought Milo's battery exploded. Look at your windows. They're blown out."

"It's a good thing our garage had windows," Winky said. "They probably prevented the walls from collapsing. That glass didn't cut you, did it?"

"I don't think so," Slick said, "Was Scooter blown out one of those back windows?"

"Scooter," Winky called out. "Are you in here?"

Scooter barked, but remained hidden under a pile of blankets in the corner of the garage. The beagle was not coming out from his hiding place as long as the lightning continued flashing across the sky.

"Scooter, I know; the sky exploded," Winky said, trying to calm the frightened beagle.

Just then, a second lightning bolt struck something in Winky's backyard.

"Our time machine was hit!" Slick yelled, and both boys ran out of the garage towards the oak tree.

Winky stopped running almost as soon as he left the garage. The giant oak tree that stood in his backyard had suffered a direct hit and was now smoldering.

"Don't go any closer," Winky said to Slick.

Only the lower portion of the oak's trunk remained intact. The rest of the giant tree was now scattered about the yard. A thin black line traced its way down what remained of the oak's trunk and stopped where the boy's wagon had been parked.

Puffs of blue smoke rose from their entry. "Our electric car is ruined," Winky said. "Just look at what that lightning bolt did to our wagon."

Slick stood there waiting for another bolt of lightning to finish him off. He couldn't take his eyes off what used to be their rusty wagon. Both it and the yard appeared to be giving off a greenish glow that filled the sky surrounding Mystic Bay. It was an eerie sight that caused Slick to freeze in his tracks.

The wagon had instantly been transformed from a rusting hulk smothered under layers electrical tape into something from a science fiction movie. The lightning had melted the electrical tape, and the gooey plastic had quickly cooled in the downpour. Now, the entire wagon was now encased in a shiny, black plastic shell. It looked like a miniature alien spaceship powered by a huge solar fan.

Milo's battery shot off its own tiny bolts of lightning that leaped directly from the battery terminals to the blades on the fan. And, it gave off a powerful hum, just like the sound made by the Mystic Bay power plant.

After the initial shock of what happened wore off, both boys were impressed by their wagon's sleek appearance. It looked stealthy and dangerous. Winky was convinced that he had created a winner.

"We are definitely going to win first prize with this entry," Winky said. "It sure looks like a time machine, doesn't it? What do you think our chances are of winning those thousand dollars now?"

"We'll win if our time machine doesn't electrocute us first," Slick said. "I don't think we should risk touching the wagon, not yet. Those sparks jumping back and forth from the battery to the fan look like they mean business."

"I never gave that a thought. I almost touched our wagon," Winky said and took three steps backwards. "You might have just saved my life. I could have been shocked."

"It was nothing, really," Slick said.

"Thanks, anyway," Winky said as he continued to study his creation. "I don't like that humming sound. Our battery didn't hum before the lightning strike."

"That's because it was dead. I wonder, did the lightning cook my dad's transformer?"

"Probably," Winky said. "Wait until my dad sees his attic fan." The rabbit pen wire was melted into a protective cage around the blades. "I hope those blades still turn. That's the only electric motor we have."

Scooter growled, and then headed straight for the wagon. Sparks or not, the beagle was determined to investigate this new contraption invading his yard.

"Scooter, get back here before that wagon turns you into a hot dog!" Winky yelled. He tried to intercept the beagle before he made contact with the wagon. Scooter was an expert at dodging humans, however. Avoiding Winky's lunge, Scooter leaped onto the plastic seat just as an arc of light whizzed past his nose.

The beagle was not intimidated. He was prepared to do battle with the tiny lightning bolts shooting out of Milo's bus battery. Nothing happened when the beagle tried to bite an elusive arc. The bolt of electricity passed harmlessly through his body on its way to the fan.

Scooter looked like a creature from another time. The beagle's fur, and ears, stood straight up from all the electrical energy stored in Milo's bus battery. The bolt of lightning had recharged it, and then some.

Once Winky saw that Scooter was able to sit in the wagon without getting electrocuted, he couldn't wait to drive his electric car around town. Slick wasn't so sure that he wanted to go on the trial run. He was still afraid of being shocked.

"Let's see if the fan works," Winky said and boldly walked over to their mutated wagon. "Wow, you can actually feel the electricity on your skin."

"I think you should come back here where it's safe," Slick said as he watched from a distance.

Winky's body started to glow, and then sparks flew out from his fingertips as he neared Slick's time machine. Once he sat down inside it, a thin layer of electricity that resembled a green neon sign outlined his entire body.

"Are you okay?" Slick asked Winky, and dared to take a few tentative steps toward the wagon. "You weren't kidding, Winky. I can feel the electricity."

"Scooter, Slick's hair is standing up," Winky said.

Scooter just nodded while sparks danced back and forth between his upright ears. Occasionally, a spark would shoot back to his tail with apparently no ill effect.

"Isn't this the wildest feeling?" Winky asked.

"It is like shuffling your feet across a rug in winter," Slick said and dared to move a little closer.

"Slick, get on your time machine. I want you to come with us on the trial run," Winky said and placed both hands on the transformer's controls.

Scooter barked, but Slick was still hesitant to get on the electrified wagon. Winky and Scooter were starting to look like green ghosts.

"Suit yourself; you had your chance. Here we go," Winky said and pushed one lever forward, just a little, just enough.

As the attic fan's blades began rotating, the green light that enveloped the wagon began pulsating. Winky's design worked, and he was about to show off his electric car to the citizens of Mystic Bay.

Slick didn't want to miss out on all the fun.

"Wait for me! I'm coming, too," Slick yelled as he ran through the electrical field surrounding the tiny wagon. "Okay, I'm on. Let's go!"

Winky pushed the red lever forward once Slick was safely on board and seated behind Scooter.

Then, something unexpected happened.

The wagon, the boys, and the beagle vanished into thin air.

"I feel a breeze, but we aren't moving," Slick said. "This isn't what I expected."

"It's the fan, silly," Winky explained. "I'll increase the power a bit; that should get us moving."

Winky again pushed on the red lever increasing the power to the fan. Sparks flew from the fan's blades and the sky went from a pale pink to a brilliant yellow. Slick kept quiet, but he really wanted off. He would have jumped, but he couldn't. The air on either side of him felt *hard*.

Scooter didn't particularly care for the sudden display of sparks shooting out from the fan and decided to hide. He forced his way onto Winky's lap for protection. Once there, the beagle buried his nose under Winky's shirt.

Slick began sensing that there was something wrong with Winky's design.

"Winky, I thought it was raining when we started," Slick said while scanning a sunny sky.

"It stopped raining. So what?" Winky tried shoving the red lever forward all the way. He was convinced that their electric car would never move forward until it could achieve full power.

Halfway down its track, the control lever struck something and refused to go any further. A thin coating of melted plastic was blocking the lever's path. When the plastic tape had melted, it quickly hardened and formed a brittle barrier. It looked like it should be easy to remove the melted tape from the control lever's path.

Unfortunately, this was not the case, and Winky's fingers were simply not strong enough to do the job.

"Stop, turn the power off," Slick said in a worried tone. "Something's wrong."

Winky ignored Slick and continued trying to force the control lever through the plastic barrier that prevented him from reaching full power. After repeated attempts to break through the thin plastic layer, he finally shut down the transformer.

Only then did Winky turn around to see what was bothering Slick.

"I thought that lightning destroyed the oak tree in your yard," Slick said and pointed off to his left.

"It did," Winky said and followed Slick's finger only to see a full set of branches, complete with leaves and two squirrels towering high above him. "Well, I thought lightning struck it; I guess I was wrong. The lightning must have hit something else."

Winky and Slick got out of their time machine and walked around the tree. It felt like the old oak tree, and the squirrels looked like the same ones Scooter had been chasing for two years. There was no doubt about it. That was Winky's oak tree, and it was still intact.

"I don't understand. It must have been that flash that made everything seem to disappear; you know, like when a flash goes off on a camera and obscures your vision," Winky said. The oak tree didn't bother him nearly as much as the melted tape blocking the path for his control lever, though. "Wait here. I'll be right back."

"Where are you going?" Slick asked.

"To the garage," Winky said. "I have to get some tools to repair your dad's transformer. Some of our electrical tape melted across the throttle's path."

"Leave the tape on there and come back outside," Slick said. "A little plastic won't hurt anything."

"But that's why we aren't moving," Winky said. "There is not enough electricity getting back to our attic fan."

"We have a bigger problem than melted plastic," Slick said. "Things just don't disappear and then suddenly reappear. That's not normal."

"I already explained what happened to the tree," Winky said. "Everything looks just like it should."

"But the only thing that vanished during that flash was the top of your oak tree," Slick said.

"Did you ever have someone take a picture of you and the flash went off?" Winky asked while he rummaged through the drawers in his father's workbench.

"Of course, everybody has," Slick said.

"Did anything in your house seem to vanish when your dad took a flash picture of you?" Winky asked.

"Yes, my mom and part of a wall disappeared," Slick replied, "but the rest of the room was still visible. It took a couple of seconds before I could see my mother again. I don't remember when the wall reappeared."

"Like I said, it was the flash of light that made the tree seem to vanish. Stop worrying about it already," Winky said. He picked up a screwdriver and hammer from his dad's workbench. "I found what I needed. Let's go."

Slick and Winky left the garage and headed back to their time machine, determined to free the red control lever and try out their entry again, this time at full power.

Winky placed the screwdriver on top of the plastic and gently tapped on it with the hammer. He could see that clearing the lever's path was not going to be as easy as it looked. This plastic had a mind of its own, and it was not about to give up without a fight.

# CHAPTER 8
## *A Shocking Reaction*

"Isn't there another way to remove that plastic?" asked Slick, now worried about the life expectancy of his father's train transformer.

"Trust me," Winky said. "This is the only way." He straddled their entry as though he were riding a futuristic four-wheeled cycle.

The plastic blocking the red lever's movement refused to break free while Winky pried at it with the screwdriver. Smiling sinisterly, Winky abandoned the screwdriver and raised the hammer high above his head into attack position. It was time to give the transformer a good whack.

"Move back while I clear this path," said Winky.

Suddenly, a miniature lightning bolt shot out from the wire mesh surrounding the fan and struck the hammer Winky was holding. The effect was immediate, and painful.

"Ouch!" Winky yelled and dropped the hammer.

The hammer bounced once on the seat and fell to the ground. Winky managed to stay on the wagon even though his hand was throbbing. Another bolt shot out from the fan, but it was after the hammer, not Winky.

"That was neat, Winky! Do it again. You looked just like Thor, the god of lightning," Slick said before noticing the look on Winky's face. "What's the matter? Does your hand hurt?"

"Of course it hurts. And now my fingers don't work," a stunned Winky said. "What exactly happened to me?"

"You must have brushed up against the wire mesh when you raised the hammer over your head," Slick said and tried to demonstrate what had happened. "You should have seen the size of the lightning bolt that shot out from the mesh. It was enormous."

"I felt it; that's enough for me," Winky said. He tried to rub some life back into his stunned hand. "And that plastic is *still* blocking our red lever's path."

"I'll take care of that plastic once and for all," Slick said and using only one finger, tentatively touched the hammer. When he didn't get shocked, he picked it up, eying the fan the whole time. He was waiting for another gigantic spark to attack the hammer. Nothing happened, but Slick kept his distance from the screen.

"Where's that screwdriver?" Slick asked.

"Over there, on the other side of the wagon," Winky said. He continued trying to massage some life back into his numb fingertips.

"I'm going to use it like a chisel. A couple of easy taps with the hammer should do the job."

Slick grabbed the screwdriver with his free hand. "Consider that plastic as good as gone," he said. "Stand back, and let a man do the job."

"Right," Winky said. "Just don't hit it too hard."

Slick ignored Winky's words of caution. Instead, he raised the hammer and hit the screwdriver as hard as he could. The single blow reminded Winky of the time Verne Randolph ran over his plastic airplane with his tractor, Betsy. There was no mistaking that crunching sound.

But it looked like their problem had been solved. The plastic that had been blocking the red control lever was now smothering two blades of grass. Winky smiled and congratulated his pal on a job well done.

"You did it," Winky said. "I thought you were going to smash that transformer into little pieces."

"It was pure luck," said Slick.

"Luck had nothing to do with it," Winky said. "You freed the path; now we can test our entry. How would you like to be the first one to drive it?"

Slick looked down at his father's transformer before replying. It looked intact and appeared to be in good working order, except for one tiny detail.

"No, you can go first," Slick said. "I'll wait over by the oak tree. You designed our entry; I think you should be at the controls on its trial run."

This was not at all like Slick. Most times, the boys would argue over who went first. The matter was usually settled by the toss of a coin. Winky became suspicious and confronted Slick before getting back on the electric car.

"What did you do to our entry?" Winky asked.

"We still have a little problem with our throttle control," Slick said. "I might have tapped the screwdriver a little too hard with the hammer—it was an accident, honest!"

"Did you crack the transformer's outer case?"

"No, but the screwdriver is stuck in the throttle path, and I can't pull it out," said Slick. "I guess I don't know my own strength."

"Move back by the fan and let me see if I can figure out how to get that screwdriver out of there," Winky said. "I hope you didn't break your dad's transformer. That is the only throttle we have."

"Hold it. I thought your fingers weren't working," said Slick.

"They were just numb from the shock. They're working now," Winky said, and demonstrated by playing an invisible piano.

Slick noticed tiny sparks shooting out from Winky's fingertips.

"Don't come any closer to me!" Slick blurted out. "You're charged with Milo's lightning bolts, and I don't want to get shocked."

"Stop acting so silly," Winky said.

"Just promise not to touch me," said Slick. "Do we have a deal?"

"It's a deal," Winky said, just as he spotted something moving out in the yard.

"What is it?" Slick asked. "What did you see?"

"Look, it's a toad," Winky said while the boys watched it hopping across the yard toward their wagon. "I'll see if I can catch it. I'm going to prove to you that my touch won't shock you."

Winky managed to corner the little toad near the trunk of the huge oak. When he reached down to pick it up, a bolt of lightning shot out from his fingertip and fried the toad instantly. A small puff of blue smoke was all that remained of the tiny creature. Even the grass nearby was scorched.

"Did you catch it?" Slick called out.

"No, it just vanished," Winky answered, electing not to tell Slick about the bolt of electricity that shot out from his finger, and the disastrous results.

"Toads are like that, elusive little buggers," Slick said. "Winky, stop chasing the toad. I managed to pull the screwdriver out of the transformer. It was magnetized, not stuck."

"Of course, it all makes sense," Winky said. "Electricity always produces a magnetic field."

Winky cautiously approached the wagon to see if its powerful electrical forces would suddenly pull him in. They didn't. He was relieved when he wasn't sucked into the wire mesh, or zapped by Milo's supercharged bus battery.

The countdown to launch began, again.

"Let's get this baby on the road. Start her up! I can't wait to be sixteen," Slick said and impatiently tried to push Winky's arm forward. "Come on, let's go!"

Both boys had already forgotten about the oak tree incident. They were too excited about testing their entry at full speed. And besides, the tree showed no signs that it had ever been struck by lightning.

Scooter, sensing an adventure was in the making, leaped into Winky's lap, knocking him back into Slick.

"Hold on," Winky said as he pushed on the red lever. "Here we go!"

This time, the lever slid forward without balking. The sun began moving, but it was going too fast. Worse yet, it was moving backwards, and so was the moon.

Something was wrong with their electric car.

# CHAPTER 9
## *The Accidental Time Machine*

"Winky, what's happening to us?" Slick asked as the sun, and then the moon, began racing backwards across the sky. "I've never seen the sun or the moon do that before. Is this the end of the world or what?"

"No, it's probably some kind of lunar eclipse," Winky said as he watched the moon chase the sun across a constantly blinking sky. "I guess the sun doesn't want to be eclipsed today."

"Look what's happening to your oak tree! This isn't a lunar eclipse," Slick shouted. "I was right. This is the end of the world!"

Winky turned his attention from the moon and checked out the giant oak in his backyard. The tree's leaves started shrinking, and then suddenly turned into tiny buds. These buds quickly disappeared back inside their branches. All that remained were bare tree limbs. Two blinks later, snow covered Winky's backyard. It, too, quickly vanished.

A season's accumulation of snow followed the buds into the past. Dried yellow leaves began swirling across the yard. Each found its place on the huge tree. Once the leaves made contact with the oak's branches, they immediately turned a dark green.

It was summer again, but only for an instant. The cycle of a year's growth continued to repeat again and again. Each time the year grew shorter, until the entire cycle took only a second to complete.

Winky and Slick's time machine worked. The oak tree started shrinking as the boys raced back in time.

"We're heading the wrong way!" Slick yelled. "I'm getting out of here before I turn into a baby!"

Slick soon discovered that he was unable to get out of Winky's creation. What appeared to be an invisible canopy kept him trapped inside the wagon. There was no escaping from their entry while it was traveling through time. The electric car was now their prison cell, and a cramped prison cell to boot.

Scooter scared himself when he barked inside Winky's time machine. His barks echoed back as though he were standing high up on Devil's Tower. The beagle agreed with Slick's earlier assessment of their situation. Frightened, he tried leaping out of Winky's entry only to smash his black nose against the invisible canopy now holding them prisoner. Scooter yelped when he bruised his nose.

"Stop our wagon right now," Slick ordered.

"But we haven't finished our trial run," Winky said. "I think we're still in my backyard."

Scooter growled at the invisible canopy.

"I wish you two would stop complaining all the time," Winky said while he watched the world outside their wagon. "Look how fast everything is changing."

"All the more reason to pull the plug on this trial run," Slick was quick to point out. "What if we run into something traveling this fast?"

"I don't think we are moving," Winky said.

"That's even worse!" Slick said. "I want out."

Scooter had finally settled down, but Slick was another matter. He was still trying to escape from their wagon. Slick couldn't see the invisible shield that held him captive. Exhausted, he finally accepted the fact that he was unable to extend his arms or legs beyond their electric car.

The mysterious barrier preventing Slick and Scooter from escaping also shielded their wagon. Nothing happening out in the backyard could make its way into where the boys were seated.

Slick was scared. So was Winky, but he would never admit it.

The periods of night and day blurred together until the sun was nothing more than a flash in the sky. It reminded Winky of the strobe light used every year in the talent show at school. The strobe was usually reserved for those students with no talent. But this was not a boring talent show they were forced to sit through before going to lunch.

Both boys watched the giant oak shrink down to the size of a sapling. It quickly disappeared into the earth as an acorn. Slick figured that he would be next and decided to keep an eye on his fingers. At the first sign of any shrinkage, he planned on pulling his dad's train wires off of Milo's tour bus battery.

"This is really something," was all that Winky could say while he watched the summer resort town of Mystic Bay slowly turn into a set from an old western movie. "You know, Slick, I believe we are going to win that thousand dollars with this time machine."

"Big deal! Stop going back in time before we disappear," Slick said and reached over Winky's shoulder when Winky did not respond fast enough to suit him. "It's time to turn this time machine off."

"Don't touch the controls," Winky warned, but Slick had already made up his mind.

There was a sickening, snapping sound when Slick yanked too hard on the red control lever. Slick knew that he had made a very big mistake.

They were not slowing down.

"I do hope that you realize what you just did," Winky said as calmly as possible. "It looks like you've broken our throttle and increased our speed."

Slick had managed to push the red lever through an additional inch of plastic before the handle snapped off in his hand. The cycle of day and night increased in speed as the boys continued traveling back in time. Thanks to Slick, Winky was unable to turn off the transformer. Their trip back in time would continue until Milo's bus battery died.

The time machine was racing out of control. All the boys could do was watch. Scooter, on the other hand, buried as much of his head as possible between the two boys. The little beagle refused to look out at his new surroundings.

"Why aren't you yelling at me?" Slick asked.

"Beats me," Winky answered as he stared outside.

"I'd feel better about this if you would yell at me," Slick said, but Winky didn't.

"Look what's happening out there," was all Winky said in a calm voice that frightened Slick more than any yelling could.

Land that had once been flat turned into rolling hills, and then into mountains. Winky and Slick were now staring out into space as they found themselves suddenly perched on the edge of a high cliff. Winky dared to look down into the deep canyon.

"This must have been what Mystic Bay looked like before it had any water in it," Winky said. "I never knew the bay was so deep."

Slick spotted movement out of the corner of his eye. A solid wall of white appeared on the horizon and was headed in their direction. "What's that, Winky?"

"Probably a cold front heading down from Canada," Winky said as he toyed with the remaining lever on the transformer. "Those aren't clouds coming this way," Slick said. "Clouds are supposed to be fluffy."

"Your brain's fluffy," Winky laughed as he scanned the horizon. "I don't see anything."

"You're looking the wrong way," Slick said, and then manually aimed Winky's head in the right direction. "Can you see it?"

"Yes," Winky whispered, and automatically reached down for the red lever that brought them to this time.

Only when he felt the jagged plastic down in the groove did Winky remember what Slick had done. There was no turning back, not without a throttle control to cut off the power to the fan. And Slick was holding the broken piece of red plastic in his hand.

"Were you looking for this?" Slick asked and held up what was left of the red lever.

Winky just shook his head and stared out at the strange looking blob heading in their direction.

Whatever it was, it started at ground level and easily touched the low-hanging clouds. The wall of white was advancing toward them at a frightening pace. Winky tried stopping the time machine using the other lever on their transformer. Nothing happened.

The boys and Scooter continued racing back in time as the wall of white advanced toward them. Slick's mysterious white blob appeared to be gaining speed.

"Now you've done it. When you snapped off the red lever, you broke something on the second control lever," Winky said to Slick. "What are we going to tell your dad when he sees this mess?"

"Who cares about an explanation at a time like this? I'll bet that's the end of the world heading this way!"

Winky watched the wall of white bulldoze its way across the countryside.

"I don't think that's the end of the world," Winky said. "But there was some kind of catastrophe on earth a long time ago. I remember reading about it in science class."

"Okay, smarty pants, what happened?" asked Slick.

"All of the dinosaurs disappeared," Winky said. "Miss Dalrymple told us that they all became extinct at the same time when an asteroid crashed into the Gulf of Mexico and formed a huge wave that drowned them."

"Baloney," said Slick. "Everyone knows that the giant asteroid that crashed on earth was carrying the Genie of Mystic Bay, and *he* was the one who got rid of the dinosaurs."

Winky just rolled his eyes and stared at the giant white blob coming their way.

Slick continued questioning Winky. "Besides, that thing out there doesn't look like a giant wave to me. What's it look like to you?"

"It looks like ice, probably a huge glacier," Winky said.

"I don't want to be in an ice cube for a thousand years," Slick said. "What are we going to do?"

"Nothing," Winky said. "We're trapped in here."

The wall of ice enveloped their time machine, but the invisible canopy prevented the boys from being crushed. The temperature inside their wagon plummeted until the boys could see their breath when they exhaled. As fast as the ice appeared, it melted. Now, with the ice gone, it was beginning to get warmer, much warmer. Suddenly, it was summertime, and the heat began to build inside their canopy.

"I don't recognize any of this; it looks more like the Amazon jungle than our Mystic Bay," Winky said. He stared out at the tropical rain forest that now surrounded their time machine.

Suddenly, Slick spotted a giant snake dangling directly over their heads.

"Get us out of here!"

The snake had to be forty feet in length, maybe longer. And it looked hungry as it slowly moved in their direction. Suddenly, the snake fell out of the giant fern it had been slithering on and landed on their time machine. It never got any closer, thanks to the invisible canopy.

Both boys watched as the snake shrank to the size of a large fishing worm, and then just disappeared into space. The time that it took the snake to finally vanish was thirty seconds. Their time machine appeared to be slowing down.

Milo's battery was running out of juice.

"I didn't particularly care for that snake," Winky said once the reptile had disappeared. "You still have that screwdriver?"

Slick nodded.

"Hand it over," said Winky. "I have to figure out some way to stop our time machine before we meet up with more gigantic creatures from the past."

Winky worked on the transformer using the screwdriver while the boys continued traveling further back in time. Mystic Bay was now a Jurassic swamp filled with exotic flowers of every imaginable color. Fluorescent pinks and purples seemed to be the color of choice. The plants appeared to dancing as Winky's time machine sped up their life cycle, in reverse. Even more impressive than the flowers were the giant ferns. They had replaced all of the trees as a source of shade in this eerie environment.

Suddenly, a series of loud thuds startled Scooter from his hiding place under Winky's left armpit. The little flea-covered beagle poked his head up from between the two boys and barked a warning to Winky.

"Easy, Scooter, I heard it, too," Winky said.

"What made that sound?" Slick asked. "Whatever

it was, it has to be nearby. I could feel the vibrations." "I'm not sure what it was," Winky said. "Maybe our time machine is acting up." He went back to work on the transformer with his screwdriver.

Finally, Winky succeeded in slowing the spinning fan blades down to a crawl. "Look, I've almost got us stopped. The sun is barely moving now." He smiled in triumph. "This screwdriver is great! It makes a perfect control lever."

Slick gave Winky a congratulatory slap on the back. "I knew you could fix it."

Just then, the booming sounds began again. The wagon bounced a little higher with each vibration, as the sounds grew increasingly louder.

Something was headed their way.

# CHAPTER 10
## *The Prehistoric Swamp*

Winky acted fast. "There, I finally figured out a way to turn off our time machine. Slick, you can open your eyes."

Slick risked a peek. "But what happened to the creature that was stalking us? I don't hear him anymore."

"Those loud thuds stopped after I cut the power to the fan. It must have been the blades making all that noise all along," Winky said, hoping his explanation would calm his pal.

"Okay, I give up. How did you stop our time machine?" Slick finally asked.

"Easy. I simply ripped off one of the wires that connected it to the battery. One hard yank was all it took to cut the battery's power to the fan."

"Do you have any idea where we are?" Slick asked.

"I guess we're lost in time." Winky shrugged his shoulders.

"Don't say that! You're the one with all the answers," Slick said with more than a hint of panic in his voice. "Which way is home? I want to go home."

"I don't know how to get home from here," Winky said, and silence filled the time machine while the boys searched the horizon for any sign of life.

Scooter finally dared to leap out of the wagon and headed for the nearest fern. A charge of electricity chased after him. It missed his tail and struck a giant fern that was now growing where the oak tree once stood. The fern sizzled away in a puff of smoke.

"How did Scooter get out of here?" Slick asked.

"The protective canopy must have disappeared when I yanked the wire off the transformer," Winky said.

"What if we see another snake?" Slick asked.

"I suggest running in the opposite direction as fast as you can," Winky said.

Now that they had lost the shield on their time machine, Winky and Slick were free to explore their new world, but would they? The swamp didn't look inviting, but the fact that it appeared to be uninhabited aroused Winky's curiosity.

There was only one thing holding him back, and Slick shared his fear.

Neither boy dared to move in the wagon because they each believed that they would be zapped by Milo's battery if they did. And they had seen what a bolt of electricity from that battery could do to a giant fern. The boys appeared to be safe as long as they remained immobile on their plastic seat.

Finally, Winky took a chance and dropped the wire he was holding. Sparks danced across the ground and then suddenly stopped. The miniature thunderstorm was over. Milo's battery was dead. Winky relaxed and took a closer look at what used to be his backyard.

"I wonder if we accidentally blew up Mystic Bay," Winky said. A chill ran up his spine, and goose bumps covered his arms.

Nothing looked familiar. The oak tree was gone, replaced by a forest of giant ferns. There were no houses, concrete walkways, or manicured yards. Only a spooky swamp was visible. This yard belonged to another time, and other beings.

"What caused those sparks?" Slick asked.

"I think Milo's battery shorted out when I dropped the wire on the ground," Winky said.

"Did you break our time machine?" Slick started to panic again at the thought of being trapped in time.

"Look who's talking. You're the one who broke the control lever. All I did was remove a wire from the transformer," Winky said. He tentatively touched the end of the wire. Nothing happened. "Well, at least we have stopped going any further back in time."

"We've stopped, period," Slick said and pointed at the sky. "Look up there. Is that normal?"

Winky followed Slick's skinny finger skyward and his heart skipped a beat. A huge *Pterodactyl* appeared to be suspended high overhead. The flying reptile looked like a giant vampire bat with a woodpecker's head. The *Pterodactyl* wasn't flying or gliding; it just hung there like a picture on a wall.

It was frozen in time.

"I better reconnect the wire to the transformer before that thing gets mad at us," Winky said when he noticed the eyes on the giant reptile. They seemed to be staring straight at him.

Then, Slick spoke up, exhibiting a sudden burst of courage.

"Wait a minute. Let's not get in too big a hurry to leave this place. We might never find it again. I think we should go exploring."

"I thought you were in a hurry to get out of here," Winky said. "Didn't you want to go home?"

"That was before you stopped time. Let's stay for a while," Slick said. "This might be interesting."

"That's okay with me, but I want to reconnect this wire before I forget where it goes," Winky said and started connecting the wire to the transformer.

"Stop, I want to check something out first. Don't connect that wire," Slick said.

"Now what are you doing?" Winky asked.

"I want to see if our protective canopy has returned," Slick said. "I don't want to smash into it." He raised his arms above his head, ever so slowly. "Okay, it's off. We can go exploring now."

"I don't think you should get out of our time machine. That's a swamp out there," Winky said to his pal. "You might sink just like my wagon did back at the landfill."

"Well, Scooter didn't sink; he didn't even make a splash," Slick said. "I'm getting out and stretching my legs before we head back home."

Winky's backyard was now covered with black water and lush vegetation that dwarfed the boys. It was strange that there were no odors. Usually a swamp smelled of rotting vegetation.

Huge leaves the size of beach umbrellas hung down from every plant in the swamp. Giant ferns had trunks that resembled snow tire treads. The sound of thunderous footsteps could no longer be heard, but the *Pterodactyl* was still overhead. And it looked hungry.

"Look, Winky, the water is frozen, but it isn't cold!" Slick tentatively tested the surface of the swamp. Then he began jumping up and down on the water to see how strong it was. "This is weird stuff. It's flexible, but you don't sink in it."

"I think that I did too good a job of stopping time when I yanked off that wire," Winky said.

"I'm sure that you'll figure out a way to start time again when we're ready to leave," Slick said.

"I hope so," Winky said. "I don't like this place. I feel like something bad is going to happen to us here."

"Stop being a party-pooper," Slick said.

Winky fell silent, but he kept an eye on the *Pterodactyl* high overhead. It still hadn't moved any closer to their time machine. Dismissing the giant bird as a threat to their safety, he dared to join his pal out on the water. This swamp water was a indeed some type of semi-solid matter.

"This is neat! Look, rubbery water," Slick said.

"I wonder if this is some form of prehistoric ice," Winky said. "It doesn't feel cold, though." He took out his phone to take a picture of the swamp.

"No, this is better than ice," Slick said. "Look, you don't slip, get wet, or anything."

Scooter ran over to greet the boys now that they were no longer inside the time machine. The beagle didn't seem to notice that he was trotting on water; he was too busy having a good time exercising his stubby legs. Then, he stopped and licked the surface.

Winky noticed this and began to worry. "What do we do if we get thirsty in this place?" he asked. "I better see if I can repair our time machine. I'm getting thirsty just thinking about getting thirsty!" He ran back to the time machine to see if he could get time moving again.

"Don't worry about it," Slick said. "We can break off a chunk of water or chew on some leaves."

To prove his point, Slick reached up and grabbed hold of a giant fern leaf. The delicate leaf refused to budge. It was locked in time, just like the *Pterodactyl*. Only the boys—and Scooter--were free to move about.

Winky reattached the wire from the battery to the transformer. "Is anything moving out there?"

"No, nothing," Slick said. He continued exploring the ancient swamp. The giant ferns offered an excellent view of the surrounding wetlands.

Since the fern's leaves were locked in time, Slick didn't have to climb up the trunk and risk injuring himself on the chisel-like bark. Instead, he simply scampered up the leaves to the top of the fern. They were solid and didn't sway; and a few even touched the ground, making the climb to the top easy. At first, the view was magnificent.

Scooter barked, expressing his irritation at being abandoned out on the swamp by both Winky and Slick. Unable to climb the fern leaf like Slick had, the beagle reluctantly trotted back to the time machine and leaped inside. There, Scooter kept bugging Winky until he finally stopped working on the transformer and started scratching the beagle behind his ears.

"I think I found out what's wrong with our time machine," Winky called out to Slick. He was reluctant to give him a status report.

"How bad is it?" Slick asked. "Can you fix our time machine and get us home in time for supper?"

"No, it looks like we might be trapped here forever," Winky said. "When I reattached the wire to the transformer, nothing happened. I thought we had a broken connection, but Milo's battery must be dead."

"Did you jiggle the screwdriver?" Slick asked.

"Yep," Winky said, and he tried to nudge it forward again. "It still doesn't work. We're stuck here."

"That might not be so bad," Slick said as he scanned the swamp from his vantage point high above the marsh. "I don't see any schools or teachers."

Slick was balancing himself on a single blade of a fern leaf. If he had tried that back in their Mystic Bay, he would have tumbled to the ground.

"I don't see any hospitals, either," Winky said. "Why don't you come down here where it's safe?"

Suddenly, Slick ducked down and motioned for Winky to be quiet. Then, he scrambled down the fern, and ran across the swamp as fast as he could. He didn't stop running until he reached their time machine.

"What happened up there?" Winky asked.

Slick leaped onto the time machine's seat and almost landed on Scooter's head. "Get us out of here, now!"

"What did you see?" Winky asked when he saw the look of terror on Slick's face. "Was it an another giant snake?"

"Worse than that," Slick gasped as he fought to catch his breath. "There is a giant dinosaur beyond the ferns." He whispered, as if talking would betray their position to the reptile. "That dinosaur saw me, and each tooth in its mouth was bigger than Scooter."

Winky wasn't sure whether to believe Slick's tale or not, but when he glanced back up at the *Pterodactyl* hanging motionless in the sky above them, he decided that it was a good time to head back to their Mystic Bay. The time machine had all of its wires reattached, and there was no reason to hang around a swamp filled with strange creatures.

"Don't panic," Winky said. "I'll get us out of here as soon as I can." He decided to give their screwdriver one more chance. Checking his wires one last time, Winky inserted the screwdriver in the transformer and pulled it back as far as possible. The fan motor hummed to life for several seconds, and then died.

"What happened?" Slick asked. "Why is the sun still overhead, and where is the moon?"

"Like I said before, Milo's battery doesn't have enough juice." Winky silently wondered how long they had to live.

Off in the distance, the boys could hear a dinosaur's booming footsteps as the fan's blades slowly rotated to a stop.

The end would be swift.

---

See Winky's swamp photo at **www.WinkyStudmire.com**. Be sure to let Winky know what kind of dinosaur tracks you think made it into his picture!

# CHAPTER 11
## *Frozen in Time*

"How long does it take to charge a battery?" a panicked Slick asked when their fan motor died.

"About an hour, but that's if we were back in my dad's garage," Winky answered. "All I'd have to do is connect Milo's dead battery to dad's battery charger."

"What about in this place?" Slick asked. "How long will it take you to recharge Milo's battery?"

"Well, batteries weren't invented when dinosaurs lived in Mystic Bay," Winky said.

"So?" Slick continued his cross-examination. "What do the dinosaurs have to do with our problem?"

"That means battery chargers weren't invented yet, either," Winky said, and the reality of their situation hit Slick.

"You don't have any idea how to charge our battery, do you?" Slick asked, and Winky shook his head.

"We might be stuck here forever," said Winky. He pushed and pulled the screwdriver through the various speed settings on the transformer. Nothing happened, not even a spark. He checked the wiring five more times before saying another word.

"I'm stumped," Winky finally said to Slick. "It looks like this swamp is going to be our new home."

"Come on, Winky, use your brain and get us out of here!" Slick wasn't ready to give up hope. "Did you check to see if one of the battery terminals came loose? Some of that lightning bolt has to be hiding inside there."

"I already told you; it's dead," Winky said. "The fan won't run without power from the battery."

"Is there any way you can get us back to our Mystic Bay on a dead battery?" Slick asked.

"No, but Milo's battery could build up another charge if we let it sit long enough," Winky said with a forced smile. "Maybe we will have enough power to move forward in time, possibly all the way back to our Mystic Bay before the battery fizzles out again."

"How long will that take?" Slick asked. "That dinosaur might still be out there waiting for us."

"We are safe for the time being," Winky said, and he got out of their time machine to stretch his legs. "Everything around us seems to be frozen in time because of the dead battery. That dinosaur won't move again until our battery builds up another charge."

"Then why are we able to move? None of this is making any sense," Slick said and scratched Scooter behind his ears.

Winky finally spoke after giving Slick's question some serious thought.

"We can move because we were inside the time machine," Winky said.

"What does being inside the time machine have to do with our being able to move?" asked Slick.

"We were traveling *through* time, not *with* it," Winky tried to explain, though he really wasn't sure why they were able to move.

Winky was only eleven years old. There was only so much his teacher could teach him, even if he was in the gifted class. And he had trouble understanding some of the technical terms in the science books he ordered through the mail.

"I know it sounds impossible, but we somehow managed to build a real time machine," Winky said. "I don't think we could ever build another one."

"Why not?" asked Slick. He joined Winky near one of the giant ferns.

"Something unexplainable happened in my backyard," Winky said. "I think the lightning bolt that struck the oak tree should be given all the credit for this piece of engineering." He stared out at the frozen swamp. "Miss Dalrymple said that most great inventions are the result of an accident. Our time machine is proof of that."

"I wish you could accidentally 'undiscover' this great invention of yours," Slick said.

"It's too late for that," Winky said.

Scooter barked a warning at the two boys, but refused to leave the time machine. Something was wrong, but Scooter couldn't put his paw on it.

Unseen by either boy, the fan's blades slowly rotated several times before the battery died again. Now, as far as Scooter was concerned, there were too many alien smells in the swamp.

"That's a good boy, Scooter; you keep a sharp eye out for any dinosaurs," Winky said. He took a quick glance around the swamp for any predators, just in case the beagle was correct. "You stay there and guard our time machine while we explore the swamp."

Scooter reluctantly agreed to stand watch. He didn't want the boys exploring the swamp, but they wouldn't listen to his warning. The little beagle curled up on the plastic seat and closed his eyes. He decided to let his ears do the watching.

Winky climbed a giant fern to see exactly what was out beyond their swamp. The view was unbelievable.

"That's a *Stegosaurus* out there! Look at the bony armor plates on his back."

The dinosaur beyond the swamp, like the *Pterodactyl* up in the sky, was also frozen in time. The boys would be safe as long as Milo's battery remained dead. Winky smiled and climbed down from the giant fern. When he reached the ground, he started out across the swamp instead of heading back to their time machine. Slick panicked.

"Where are you going?" Slick asked when he noticed Winky walking in the wrong direction. "Who knows what might be out there?"

"I thought you wanted to explore. Come on, I want to check out that *Stegosaurus* up close," Winky said. "Don't worry; it's frozen in time like everything else."

"I never thought of time as being something so cold," Slick said. He quickly joined his pal on the edge of the ancient swamp. "Okay, I'm here, but I'm not going to touch that dinosaur. He looks angry."

"I dare you to touch him," Winky said.

"I happen to like my fingers," Slick said.

"I'm telling you that nothing is going to happen as long as Milo's battery is dead," Winky said.

The swamp resembled the giant mural hanging in the Mystic Bay Museum. There was no wind, no smells, and no sounds. But unlike the mural in the museum, all of the images were three-dimensional, and some were downright scary.

The boys walked on until they reached the dense growth that marked the end of the swamp. Winky looked over his shoulder one last time to make certain that he would be able to find his way back to their time machine. It looked tiny compared to the huge vegetation in the swamp.

Winky wasn't sure, but he thought that the fan blades on their time machine had shifted slightly. One blade had been pointing straight up the last time he looked. Now, none of the blades were pointing up toward the sky. But nothing appeared to be rotating.

"Are the blades on our fan turning?" Winky asked Slick before continuing deeper into the fern forest.

Slick studied the blades for a long time. "I don't think so," he finally said. "It's the glare off of the water that makes them look like they are shimmering. No, they are definitely not rotating."

"You are probably right about the glare," Winky said, and the boys continued exploring the vast swamp and the surrounding marshland. The ground was spongy.

"That bird looks like it's lower than it was the last time we checked," Slick said to Winky, as he glanced up at the sky. The *Pterodactyl* had indeed dropped a good fifty feet closer to their time machine, and that its claws were open to attack position. But it appeared to be once again frozen in time.

"That's probably because we are looking at it from a different angle over here on the land," Winky said, and dismissed the change in position as an optical illusion.

"I don't know about that. It looks lower to me," Slick said, but Winky had something else on his mind.

"Let's check out that dinosaur before it turns into a fossil," Winky said as he came dangerously close to the huge reptile.

Now, neither boy could see the blades on the fan begin turning, stop for a second, and then start rotating again.

Milo's battery was ever so slowly recharging itself under the warm prehistoric sun.

In his haste to see the dinosaur up close, Winky forgot to move the screwdriver into the "off" position before heading out across the swamp. It was a careless error, one that could cost the boys dearly.

"Look at the size of this dinosaur," Winky said while he kicked its leg like a man checking the tires on a used truck.

"I think you should move back a little," Slick said. "What if it would fall over on you?"

"It can't; it's locked in time," Winky said and gave the dinosaur rough pat.

Slick couldn't believe what he was seeing. He could have sworn he saw the dinosaur's head move ever so slightly, and then begin slowly turning toward his pal.

"Winky, look out!" Slick shouted when the dinosaur suddenly lurched around to see what was attacking its hind leg. "It's going to clobber you!"

# CHAPTER 12
## *The Chase Begins*

Oblivious to the attack happening deep in the swamp, Scooter snored peacefully inside the time machine. An occasional flea would interrupt his dreams, causing him to gnaw at one of his ribs until the itching stopped. All the while, Scooter's eyes never opened. He preferred the vision of tasty bones in his dreams to the reality of a lifeless swamp.

And so, Scooter didn't bother to look back when the attic fan produced a faint humming sound. The fan's blades were barely rotating, but their movement was enough to bring the prehistoric Mystic Bay back to life.

Out in the ancient swamp, both boys panicked when the eighteen-foot *Stegosaurus* suddenly became unfrozen, looked back at Winky, and then decided to get rid of the pest that had kicked him.

"Look out for the dinosaur's tail!" Slick shouted, but Winky was too close to the midsection of the dinosaur to detect the movement. He didn't see the dinosaur's head move, or its giant armored tail whip around to strike whatever had pestered it.

Suddenly the *Stegosaurus* froze into a statue-like pose again, just like the *Pterodactyl* above them.

Scooter heard Slick yell and jumped to his feet. Sensing danger out in the swamp, he barked a warning to the boys. Nothing was attacking him, but the beagle knew that something wasn't right. The foul swamp odors were back.

"We're still alive, Scooter! Go back to sleep," Winky yelled to the beagle. "Everything's okay."

Slick, was far from okay. In fact, he looked like he was going to be sick. He stumbled and almost tripped over a rock while trying to back away from the *Stegosaurus*.

"Slick, what's wrong?" Winky asked. "Maybe you should sit down and take a break."

"That dinosaur just tried to whap you in the head," Slick said. "It was swinging its tail through the air like an ax."

"Did you drink some swamp water?" Winky asked.

"How could I? It's frozen, remember?"

"You've got to stop making up stories like that," Winky said. "It's no wonder that you're always getting yelled at in school."

"I didn't make it up!" Slick said. "I'm telling you that dinosaur's tail moved."

"Then why didn't it hurt me?" Winky asked.

Slick didn't have an answer. "Maybe I am seeing things," he said. "I do feel a little queasy."

"Settle down and tell me what you thought you saw," Winky said while he continued his dinosaur examination. "I wonder what made Scooter bark like that. He must have had another nightmare."

"Knowing Scooter, he probably sat on a bare wire and thought a giant prehistoric flea was attacking him." Slick laughed, and Winky nodded in agreement.

Slick's guess had been fairly accurate regarding Scooter's outburst. While the beagle was snoozing inside their time machine, his tail had brushed against the metal part of the screwdriver.

Scooter's tail shorted out the electrical charge feeding the fan, causing it to stop rotating. In addition to saving Winky from the dinosaur, it had also given the beagle quite a jolt.

After Slick calmed down, he told Winky how close he had come to getting himself clobbered by the dinosaur's armored tail. Winky listened and studied the huge reptile, still convinced that Slick was seeing things.

The dinosaur resembled a huge plastic toy. Its skin was hard like the merry-go-round animals he rode down at the annual Mystic Bay summer carnival.

"Are you sure it moved?" Winky asked.

"I think it did," Slick said. "Doesn't it look like it's in a different pose now?" The *Stegosaurus* was indeed now in an attack stance with its tail slightly elevated.

Just then, Scooter barked at a cat in his dream and flipped over on his side. At the same time, his hind leg struck the screwdriver on the transformer, moving it slightly forward. Nothing happened inside the time machine, but it was an entirely different story out in the swamp.

"Watch out!" Slick yelled and pulled Winky back so hard that they both fell to the ground.

The dinosaur's tail smashed into the soft earth where Winky had been standing only seconds earlier. The force of the blow knocked a giant fern twenty feet deeper into the swamp. The black water was no longer solid, and the fern quickly sank out of sight. The boys now had to contend with their own nightmare.

"Thanks," Winky said when he jumped to his feet.

"That dinosaur sure looks unfrozen to me," Slick said.

"Yep. It's alive, hungry, and mad at us," Winky said, before shouting "Run!" as loudly as he could.

The sound of the dinosaur's tail smashing the ground was deafening. It was enough to convince Winky that Slick had been correct. Both boys ran through the swamp with a lumbering *Stegosaurus* chasing after them.

"I thought that dinosaurs only ate vegetables," Slick said while they waded waist deep through the black swamp water.

"Why don't you go back and tell him that he's supposed to be a vegetarian?" Winky said, suddenly realizing that he was soaked. "What happened to our frozen swamp?"

"I think it melted."

The boys were having difficulty making any headway. They had to wade in the swamp water now instead of walking on it, and the dinosaur was closing in on them. On land, they might have stood a chance of escaping, but this dinosaur was at home in the swamp.

"Where did our time machine go?" Winky shouted.

"It's over there," Slick said, and he managed to grab Winky just before the dinosaur hit him with his tail.

The water exploded from the impact, sending a wave rippling across the swamp. Luckily, the wave also carried the boys a safe distance from the *Stegosaurus* that was chasing them. Now, they were in shallower water.

"Thanks," gasped Winky. "I never saw its tail coming at me. It could have broken my arm."

"You can thank me later; keep running!" Slick said. "You need to fix that time machine and get us out of here!"

The boys continued running toward their time machine.

In addition to the *Stegosaurus* coming to life, the *Pterodactyl* continued its downward glide out of the prehistoric sky. The flying reptile had managed to grab a hold of their time machine with its claws. The weight of Winky's invention must have surprised it.

The *Pterodactyl* appeared to be having a great deal of difficulty taking off with its new prey. The rear wheels of the time machine skimmed across the surface of the swamp. Even though the *Pterodactyl* was neither gaining nor losing altitude, the boys were in serious danger of losing their time machine.

Winky was the first to realize this. "We are going to be trapped in time forever!" He watched with despair as the *Pterodactyl* struggled to fly off.

"Maybe he won't eat it," Slick said.

Slowly, the *Pterodactyl* started gaining altitude until the last of their time machine was out of the water. The boys could do nothing to save Scooter, or their wagon. In a few more seconds, the *Pterodactyl* would clear the swamp and probably disappear forever.

Slick suddenly pointed skyward. "Look, the *Pterodactyl* is losing altitude. Our wagon must be too heavy for him. He's running out of gas."

Winky Studmire, Time Traveler, saw that there would be only one chance to return to the Mystic Bay he knew and loved. Without hesitating, he started running across the shallow water. He hoped that he could reach his time machine before it was too late.

Slick ran after his pal, terrified of being left behind. He didn't want to lose their time machine either, but he was even more concerned about being attacked by the dinosaur that was still hot on their tail.

The lumbering *Stegosaurus* had almost caught up with the boys. Each of the dinosaur's steps equaled at least fifteen of theirs. Just as it was about to attack Slick, the dinosaur froze into another statue-like pose.

Time had once again stopped in the boys' prehistoric Mystic Bay.

The boys, however, continued racing across the frozen water. Winky was surprised that the water did not trap them when it turned back into its semisolid form, but he was thankful for the break.

"The fan blades have stopped rotating again. The battery must have used up its charge," Winky said. He reached for an axle. "Quick, grab a hold of our wagon and whatever you do, don't let go."

"But it's not going anywhere," Slick said, and looked back to see where the *Stegosaurus* was once he had a firm grip on the wagon.

The dinosaur was still posed statue-like, ready to attack a prey that had already moved to safer ground. "We're safe. Everything is frozen in time again." Winky sighed. "I wonder how long this will last."

"How long do we have to hold on like this?" Slick asked as he grabbed the rear axle of the time machine.

"Until the *Pterodactyl* lets go of our wagon," Winky said.

Just then, his attic fan roared back to life.

This time the blades rotated several times before coming to a stop. The *Pterodactyl* climbed higher into the prehistoric sky leaving the charging *Stegosaurus* far behind. Both boys watched the dinosaur give one last lunge as it tried to bite off Slick's right leg.

Both Winky and Slick almost lost their grip on the wagon's rear axle. Then, the *Pterodactyl* was once again frozen in the sky above the ancient swamp. The boys were too high in the air to even consider letting go of their wagon.

Little did they know, something else had been stalking them in the prehistoric Mystic Bay.

While they clung to the rear axle, neither boy noticed the *Tyrannosaurus* that had been charging toward them from the far end of the swamp. Both boys had been too busy trying to rescue the wagon that was their only hope of ever returning home.

The *Tyrannosaurus* was three times the size of the *Stegosaurus*. And unlike the *Stegosaurus*, the *Tyrannosaurus* had a huge head and a mouthful of sharp enameled spikes that served as teeth. To make matters worse, it was fast and walked erect on two feet.

Paleontologists would not have been surprised to learn that neither Winky nor Slick were able to spot the giant dinosaur that was stalking them. Its camouflage was perfect. The green skin perfectly matched the dark green of the swamp's vegetation.

Winky and Slick were heading straight for the carnivore. With the next turn of the attic fan's blades, the boys could be eaten alive.

Their lives depended on the strength of the *Pterodactyl's* wings. And, in addition to the wagon and Scooter, the flying reptile now had to carry two growing boys.

---

Winky didn't realize it at the time, but he recorded a video while he and Slick were being chased by the dinosaur. Check it out at **www.WinkyStudmire.com**.

# CHAPTER 13
*Trapped*

"Wow, we can see all of prehistoric Mystic Bay from up here," Slick said. "Look, more dinosaurs. What kind are they?"

"I'm not sure. I think that's a herd of *Sauropods*," Winky said and started counting. "Miss Dalrymple told us that all dinosaurs with long necks and tails belong to the family of *Sauropods*. So far, I've counted twenty of those giants out there."

Slick stared at the strange landscape beneath him. Nothing looked familiar. Future trees were nothing more than tiny weeds. Giant ferns dominated this forest. The ferns surrounded the swamp for as far as he could see.

Slick was also having a hard time holding on, to the rear axle of their time machine, especially with a dinosaur below that wanted him for lunch. He knew that no one would believe his tale if he ever made it back to his Mystic Bay.

The fan blades then turned without any warning. They made one complete revolution. This sudden movement caused Winky's grip to tighten on the wagon's axle. Then, Slick spotted something.

"Look, there's a hill," Slick said, pointing it out with his foot as it slid directly beneath them before time once again came to a halt. "That's strange; I don't remember seeing a hill in the middle of the swamp, do you?"

"I'm not so sure that's a hill," Winky said.

"It looks like one to me," Slick said. "I think I can touch it with my foot."

"I wouldn't do that if I were you," Winky said.

"I'm losing my grip," said Slick. "I have to give my fingers a break before I fall into the swamp."

Fortunately for the boys, their time machine began losing altitude every time the *Pterodactyl* flapped its wings. With the last spin of the blades, it dropped low enough for Winky and Slick to step on a knoll out in the middle of the swamp. They took this opportunity to give themselves a much-needed break.

"My fingers don't want to let go," Winky said.

"Mine are numb. I don't think I could have held on much longer," Slick said when he let go of the wagon. "It's a good thing we found this hill. I thought I was a goner. There, that's better."

Slick was careful to keep one hand near the wagon's rear axle, just in case Winky's unpredictable fan suddenly sprang to life. The fan was the only thing Slick could count on in this world filled with giant ferns and dinosaurs.

Winky took a bigger chance and dared to let go of the wagon with both hands. While standing on Slick's hill, he scanned the swamp for predators. Aside from the giant ferns and frozen *Stegosaurus*, the swamp appeared to be deserted. Winky never thought about checking the hill on which he was standing.

"You're too far away from the wagon," Slick warned his pal before the fan came back to life.

"Thanks for the heads up," Winky said.

"You better keep one hand on that axle, just to play it safe," Slick said. "I don't want to get stuck traveling through time all by myself."

Heeding Slick's warning, Winky moved closer to the wagon and kept one hand up near the rear axle, just in case his attic fan started spinning again. But he did not grab a hold of it; his fingers were too tired. Instead, Winky shook his hands as he tried to get the blood circulating back into his fingertips. He looked like a baby bird learning how to fly.

Below, and off to their right, was the *Stegosaurus*. It appeared to have given up the chase just when it looked like it might have captured the boys. The dinosaur looked frightened as it stood there frozen in time. Winky thought this to be odd; the boys posed no threat to the huge reptile.

But then he supposed that if he were the one being turned on and off by a time machine, he, too, would be frightened. As Winky continued his pan of the swamp, he turned and came face-to-face with the largest eyeball he had ever seen.

Worse yet, it blinked.

Winky heard the fan's motor come to life.

Out of nowhere, lightning began flashing across the sky.

Winky screamed and leaped up off of the nose of the giant *Tyrannosaurus*. The small knoll hadn't been a hill at all; it was the giant head of a bigger dinosaur in the swamp! It was easy to mistake this dinosaur for swampy land. Both the land and the dinosaur's body were covered with a slimy, green substance that resembled moss. And it smelled like rotting vegetation.

Time became a blur as the adrenalin rush took control of both Winky and Slick's bodies. Slick closed his eyes and clung to the time machine. Winky accidentally kicked the huge dinosaur in the eye when he leaped up to grab the wagon's axle. The *Pterodactyl* had once again come to life and was now struggling to gain altitude to avoid being eaten.

The *Tyrannosaurus* moved faster than the *Stegosaurus* as it charged after the boys. Winky's other foot accidentally scraped across the dinosaur's eye a second time as the time machine slowly dragged him into the future. The huge reptile let out a deafening roar and blindly took a swipe at the boys.

Slick screamed.

The *Pterodactyl* continued towing their time machine higher into the prehistoric sky. Fear of being eaten alive was driving the flying reptile to new heights.

Then, the flapping wings above their wagon became sluggish. The *Pterodactyl* looked like it was flying in slow motion. Even the *Tyrannosaurus* appeared to be winding down, but it continued lumbering after them.

"I think our bird's had it," a panicked Slick shouted as he curled his legs up to avoid being eaten by the *Tyrannosaurus*. "Winky, that dinosaur's closing the gap between us. What are we going to do?"

"Hang on," Winky said. "There's nothing else we can do. We're too high above the swamp to risk letting go." He paused. "Listen, do you hear that?"

"Hear what?" Slick asked. "All I hear is you."

"Precisely," Winky said and looked up.

Winky couldn't hear the fan's motor humming, but the blades were still spinning. In a few seconds, the swamp and everything in it would once again be frozen in time. It would be close, as the *Tyrannosaurus* only needed a few more seconds to catch up with them.

"That dinosaur is going to eat us," Slick screamed and closed his eyes.

"You can open your eyes. I think we are safe for now," Winky said when both the *Tyrannosaurus* and the *Pterodactyl* again froze into a familiar pose.

"What makes you think that?" Slick asked as he opened one eye. "Look at the size of those choppers."

"Check out the blades on our fan," Winky said.

"So, we aren't out of the woods yet, are we?" Slick asked while he gazed at the blades on the time machine.

"I think you mean swamp," Winky corrected his pal. "There won't be any woods for a million years."

"Swamp, woods; who cares what you call it?" Slick asked. "You know what I meant."

"You're right," Winky said. "We are still in a lot of trouble. But it could be worse."

The fan's blades had stopped rotating, and so did time in ancient Mystic Bay. Nothing was moving except Winky, Slick, and the wagon. Scooter still hadn't budged since the *Pterodactyl* grabbed their wagon.

Winky couldn't tell if the beagle was sleeping or had died of shock when he saw the flying reptile attack their time machine. A loud snore from inside the modified wagon answered that question.

"How can he sleep through all this?" Slick asked.

"Scooter can fall asleep anywhere," Winky said. "He once took a snooze on Verne Randolph's tractor, Betsy."

"What's the big deal about that?" Slick asked.

"Verne was driving through Mystic Bay when it happened," Winky said. "Scooter never woke up."

"Get out of here," said Slick.

It felt good talking about their Mystic Bay, the one that had a real forest. It also reminded Slick that they were trapped, stranded in a world filled with predators.

Winky had other thoughts on his mind.

Milo's bus battery appeared to be drained of electricity. It would take some time for it to build up another charge. Winky figured that they had at least thirty minutes to relax, maybe even check out the *Tyrannosaurus* up close--not that it was far away.

After the thirty minutes were up, it would be impossible to predict exactly when the fan's blades would start rotating again. Their motor followed no regular pattern for starting or stopping, other than the minimum time needed to recharge the battery.

"We're safe for the time being," Winky said. "Neither dinosaur is chasing us, and our flying reptile hasn't flapped his wings for a while."

Even though the predators in their surroundings were once again frozen in time, Slick did not share Winky's assessment of their situation. He could still see both dinosaurs, and the fact that he was dangling above the *Tyrannosaurus'* gaping mouth terrified him.

Precarious would best describe his predicament. To Slick, this was a living nightmare. "Okay, what's bugging you?" Winky asked.

"For starters, my hands are killing me," Slick said, but he didn't let go of the axle.

"My hands hurt, too," Winky said.

"What exactly makes you think that we are safe up here?" Slick asked. "We are too high above the swamp to risk letting go. The fall alone might kill us."

"You could be right about that," Winky said.

Winky followed Slick's gaze downward while they both dangled beneath their time machine. Directly below was the *Tyrannosaurus* with its jaws open. It was waiting for one of them to fall into its mouth.

Above the boys, on the plastic seat, Scooter was still out cold and showed no signs of waking, despite the boys' yelling.

"My fingers are getting tired," Winky finally said and tried to think of a way to save himself from the dinosaur's waiting jaws. "There has to be a way to escape those teeth. Each one is over a foot long."

"I wouldn't count on finding a way in time. I'm losing my grip," Slick said as he fought to maintain his hold on the axle. "I don't think I can hold on much longer. What are we going to do?"

"Don't let go until I tell you," Winky said. "I've got another plan, and this one just might work."

Before Winky could explain his plan, the fan blades on the time machine began turning. The battery had built up another charge too soon. Life returned to the ancient swamp. Lightning bolts again danced across the sky. Their *Pterodactyl* was tiring and began losing altitude. Below, the *Tyrannosaurus* relentlessly chased them through the swamp and beyond.

The huge dinosaur bulldozed his way through the giant ferns blocking his path. Nothing stood in its way, not even a giant boulder that seemed to appear out of nowhere in the lush vegetation of the swamp. The *Tyrannosaurus* simply bowled over the huge rock, as if it were a pebble. The dinosaur's massive frame succeeding in breaking the boulder with a loud *crack*. The noise was loud enough to even wake Scooter up.

All of a sudden, the lightning stopped.

The boys' nightmare, however, had only just begun. Slick was the first to feel the breath of the *Tyrannosaurus* when it tried to swallow them, the time machine, and the *Pterodactyl*, all in one gulp. A long reptilian tongue shot out to collect its prey. When the dinosaur's slimy tongue narrowly missed its target, the time machine's fan stopped once more.

Winky knew they needed to act fast.

"Quick! Get on the dinosaur's tongue before the battery builds up another charge. I'll climb up his teeth and get in our time machine." Winky started scrambling up the mouthful of jagged teeth that only seconds earlier was ready to rip him to shreds.

Slick, on the other hand, hadn't moved. This was not the plan he wanted to hear.

"Have you lost your mind?" Slick asked. "That's exactly what this dinosaur wants me to do, climb into its mouth. He's going to turn me into hamburger!"

"Not if we leave him in the past and return to our Mystic Bay," Winky said, and just the way he said it made Slick obey. "Follow me back to the time machine if you don't want to stand on the dinosaur's tongue. It really doesn't matter one way or the other. We aren't going to be here that long."

"Now that's what I call a plan," Slick said. "Let's get out of this swamp."

The boys used the long teeth of the *Tyrannosaurus* as a stepladder. Carefully, they made their way up from the rear axle to the transformer on their time machine. The dinosaur's tongue remained wet and began dissolving the boys' clothing whenever they made contact with it. The reptile's saliva was potent.

"That foul smell is acid. Whatever you do, don't touch that tongue with your hands," Winky said while he managed to pull himself closer to the controls. "I wonder why the acid didn't solidify like the swamp water. It should have; everything else in this place did. Do you think it contains antifreeze?"

"Who cares? Just get us out of here as fast as you can," said Slick. "I don't like being inside a mouthful of teeth, especially when they are after me."

Scooter yelped when Winky sat down on his tail too hard. The little beagle jumped to his feet, but he did not make any attempt to leap out of the time machine. He sensed that danger was nearby.

"Sorry, Scooter, but I haven't got time to explain," Winky said. "Now, what was I doing?"

"Do you smell something burning?" Slick asked.

"Yes," Winky said and turned around.

Scooter started barking once Slick joined them in the time machine. Slick's one shoe was smoking from its brief encounter with the dinosaur's tongue.

"I think you're on fire," Winky said to his pal.

"Don't just sit there; help me!" Slick yelled.

Smoke quickly filled the inside of the dinosaur's mouth. Choking, the boys were forced to shove their heads out between the gaps in the dinosaur's teeth in order to breathe. It was a dangerous maneuver.

Slick's shoe continued puffing smoke for another twenty seconds before it finally stopped. Winky guessed that the treated leather had somehow neutralized the dinosaur acid. Slick believed him.

"I think it's safe to go back inside," Winky said once the smoke had cleared. "Come on, Slick, stop goofing around."

"My head's stuck," said Slick. "I'm trapped."

"Shut your mouth and pull back hard."

Slick forced his head back through the giant teeth. "Ouch! You made me break my ear."

"You'll live," Winky said. "Sit down."

Pushing the screwdriver forward had brought them to the past, so once the boys were safely in their seats, Winky pulled the screwdriver all the way back in order to travel to the future. Nothing happened. They remained trapped in the dinosaur's mouth. Milo's battery was dead. Scooter barked and Slick added his two-cent's worth of advice. Winky just sat there.

"I agree, Scooter," Slick said while petting the frightened beagle. "I don't think Winky ever had a plan. He was just trying to make us feel good."

"Did we bring any extra wire with us?" Winky suddenly asked. "I need more wire to make this work."

"No, but I brought your mother's aluminum clothesline with us," Slick said. "I wrapped it around the wire mesh since the wire from my dad's train set wasn't strong enough." He listened for any signs of life in the *Tyrannosaurus*, the *Pterodactyl*, or the fan. "Winky, did you hear something?"

"Like what?" Winky asked.

"I think I heard the electric motor," said Slick. "Oh, no--the fan's blades are beginning to turn again!"

"Hold on, and don't let go!" Winky shouted.

# CHAPTER 14
## *Inside the T-rex*

"Watch out for those teeth!" Slick yelled.

Surprisingly, the *Tyrannosaurus* ignored the time machine inside its mouth. The huge beast gave a sudden lunge upward when the fan's blades started rotating. The dinosaur wasn't after the boys. The *Tyrannosaurus* had acquired a taste for *Pterodactyl*s.

Now, the flying reptile, the time machine, and all of its occupants, were trapped inside the dinosaur's cavernous mouth. The wagon was resting on the reptile's tongue, but the *Pterodactyl* wasn't so lucky.

The stench inside the dinosaur's mouth made breathing all but impossible. When the *Tyrannosaurus* opened its jaws to get a firmer grip on the struggling *Pterodactyl*, Winky ripped a wire off Milo's tour bus battery. Huge jaws continued clamping down on the flying reptile until the blades once again came to a halt.

Time had once again stopped in the prehistoric world of Mystic Bay. Nothing was moving. The boys were safe again for the time being, and so was Scooter.

The same could not be said for the *Pterodactyl*. It had fallen out of the *Tyrannosaurus'* jaws and was once again suspended in midair. It was bleeding, but not badly. Several of the *Tyrannosaurus'* sharp teeth had punctured one of its wings. Some skin had been torn open, but other than that, the bird-like reptile did not appear to be seriously injured. It could survive.

"That could have been one of us," Slick whispered. "Those teeth sure are sharp."

Scooter barked, startling both boys. Winky comforted the little dog.

"Don't worry, Scooter, we're safe for as long as we want. I've stopped time permanently in this Mystic Bay. No more surprises; I promise." Winky held up a crumpled wire for the beagle to see.

"What's that?" Slick asked when he spotted the red wire. "What did you do to our time machine?"

"I pulled a wire off in order to stop time, that's all," Winky said.

Scooter barked and became more daring when the *Tyrannosaurus* didn't move. The beagle shared Winky's confidence and growled daringly at the huge teeth. Slick still had his doubts and expressed them.

"Big deal, so you stopped time. We're still trapped inside this dinosaur's mouth," Slick said.

It was true; they were in a prison of sorts. The dinosaur's mouth had become their jail cell. Thick bars of yellow enamel prevented them from escaping. Only Scooter could squeeze his entire body through the gaps in the giant reptile's teeth, and he wasn't interested in doing so any time soon.

"Look on the bright side; it can't possibly get any worse than this," Winky said as he studied their predicament. "Our situation can only get better."

Suddenly, the wagon shifted.

Slick automatically assumed the worst. "I think Scooter's barking woke up our dinosaur."

"That's impossible. Our fan doesn't have a power source," Winky said, and then looked around to see if something else was causing their time machine to move.

"Then why are we sliding backwards?" Slick asked.

"There's the problem," Winky said, pointing toward the front of the wagon. "The dinosaur didn't come back to life; we've simply lost our anchor."

"I didn't know that we had an anchor on our time machine," said Slick.

"It's just a figure of speech. The *Pterodactyl* was our anchor," Winky said.

Ever since the *Pterodactyl* had released its grip on their time machine, the little wagon began to slowly drift across the slippery tongue of the *Tyrannosaurus*.

"I don't like this," Slick said and started to get off the time machine. Most of the acid inside the dinosaur's mouth was now a semisolid and rendered harmless. Slick discovered this when he stepped on the reptile's tongue again. This time, his shoe didn't catch on fire. No smoke or fumes filled the inside of the dinosaur's cavernous mouth.

Slick still panicked nonetheless. "Winky, we are still moving!" He leaped off the wagon a second time. "Come on, Winky, you've got to get out of that thing before it disappears down the dinosaur's throat."

Winky refused to get out of his wagon. "I can't let that happen to my time machine."

Slick reluctantly jumped back on the wagon to join his pal.

This time, Slick's sudden movement caused the wagon to slide closer to the dinosaur's left row of teeth. Finally, he managed to do something right, even though it was accidental. Winky saw what was happening and decided to give a new plan a try.

Winky grabbed a dinosaur tooth when his time machine made contact with the bottom row of teeth. He did this while trying to hold on to their wagon with his other hand. It was clear that he needed more hands. Winky began barking out orders to Slick.

"Let's give it one last shot before we abandon our time machine," Winky said. "Grab a tooth while I try to wedge a wheel in between one of its teeth."

Slick saw what Winky planned to do and quickly joined in the effort. They had to prevent their time machine from sliding into the dinosaur's stomach. The reptile's digestive acid had not yet changed into a semisolid. The wagon would dissolve upon contact, and so would their chances of ever seeing their Mystic Bay.

Scooter barked out a suggestion. He even tried to help the boys by tugging on the wagon's handle. The beagle slipped and almost slid down the dinosaur's throat. Terrified of being swallowed alive, Scooter jumped back in the wagon. This time, he stayed there.

"Man, this dinosaur has bad breath," said Slick.

"Don't just stand there! I need you up here," Winky said, and then squeezed his head out between two dinosaur teeth to fill his lungs with fresh swamp air.

"I can't do it," said Slick, too afraid to move. "The dinosaur's tongue is too slippery! I might fall."

The stomach acid was giving off a pungent odor that made breathing difficult inside the dinosaur's mouth. Winky thought that he recognized the smell. It seemed a lot like battery acid.

He had an idea, but it was a long shot.

"Slick, hold on to the time machine. I'm going to climb down to the attic fan and unwind the aluminum wire wrapped around the wire mesh," Winky said and waited for Slick to get a better grip on both the dinosaur's tooth and the wagon before he dared to let go of anything. "Well? Do you have it?"

"I've got it," said Slick. "You can let go."

"Make sure that you don't do the same," Winky said.

"Be careful where you step; that tongue's really slippery," Slick said, closed his eyes, and waited.

Slick didn't want to see his pal fall into the dinosaur's stomach. But Winky had no difficulty making his way down to the fan and the clothesline. He used the dinosaur's teeth for a ladder and climbed down until he reached the rear of the wagon. Once there, he began removing the coils of aluminum wire.

It was a good thing Winky placed Slick in charge of attaching the screen to their time machine. As usual, Slick had used far more material than was needed to do the job. After uncoiling less than half of the clothesline, Winky saw there was enough aluminum wire for his plan, and some left to hold the wire mesh in place.

Scooter questioned everything while Winky worked on the fan. Even though the beagle could not help the boys, he wanted to know what they were planning.

"We need this aluminum wire in order to get back to our Mystic Bay," Winky said, and Scooter nodded, even though he had no idea what aluminum was.

"What are you planning to do with that clothesline?" Slick asked.

"First, I'm going to anchor our wagon to a tooth so it won't slide any further down the dinosaur's throat." He started removing more coils of wire from the mesh that surrounded their fan.

"You better hurry up. My fingers are getting tired," Slick said. "I don't think I can hold on much longer."

"I'm coming up," Winky said. "Don't let go."

"I'm trying, Winky," an exhausted Slick said.

Winky stopped uncoiling the wire and started bending it back and forth until it snapped. Next, he wrapped one end of the clothesline to the time machine's front wheels. Then, he started climbing up the side row of teeth, uncoiling the wire as he climbed.

"Here, wrap this wire around that tooth," Winky said and handed Slick a length of wire.

"You're kidding me," Slick said. "I'm holding onto a dinosaur tooth with my left hand and the time machine with my right. I only have two hands."

"Okay, I'll wrap the wire around the tooth; you just concentrate on not letting go," Winky said. He then began climbing until he finally reached the dinosaur's huge front teeth. "This should anchor our wagon."

When Winky finished wrapping the wire around the tooth, he relaxed and let go of the remaining length of clothesline. It fell into the pool of stomach acid. Despite the fact that everything else was frozen in time, the dinosaur's stomach acid refused to turn into a semisolid. The effect was immediate.

"Ouch," Slick yelled and quickly let go of their time machine. "Winky, what did you do?"

"Nothing, honest," Winky said and watched in horror as the time machine started sliding down the dinosaur's cavernous throat. "Grab hold of a wheel!"

"No way--that wagon shocked me!" said Slick.

Winky grabbed a wheel and was immediately zapped. He let go and watched the time machine slide further back into the dinosaur's throat. Finally, the slack in the wire was taken up, and the aluminum wire held. The time machine came to a halt after sliding only a few feet.

The coil of wire that had been touching the acid was now suspended several inches above the pool of digestive juices. The time machine had taken up the slack and pulled the clothesline free of the acid.

"That was close," Winky said. He studied the aluminum clothesline that disappeared down the *Tyrannosaurus'* throat and began working on his next plan.

Winky was convinced that he could charge Milo's battery using the aluminum clothesline and the dinosaur's stomach acid. Once the battery was fully charged, the boys would escape back to their Mystic Bay before the dinosaur could swallow them.

But it was just a theory.

# CHAPTER 15
## *The Makeshift Battery Charger*

"I think time travel stinks, and so does our dinosaur's breath," said Slick. He poked his head through one of the gaps between its teeth. "Scooter, come up here. The air's better, and so is the company."

"Ha, ha," Winky said. "You're a real comedian."

Scooter ignored both boys and squatted lower against the wire mesh. The little beagle didn't want anything to do with those huge chunks of enamel. When Slick came back inside to get him, Scooter growled.

"Fine, stay down there; see if I care," Slick said, and then shoved his head out through a different gap.

Winky took a break and joined Slick. The pair looked like two inmates when their heads poked out between the huge gaps. Though Winky refused to admit it, the swamp air was better than breathing dinosaur breath. The acid fumes from the reptile's stomach burned his eyes and made breathing difficult.

"Is that an *Allosaurus* over there?" Winky asked and pointed it out for Slick. "It's the one near that giant fern off to your right. Can you see it?"

"No, all I see is a big dinosaur," said Slick.

"I was referring to the big dinosaur," Winky said.

"That's not what you called it," said Slick. "I wonder if he knows that's his name."

"I don't think so," Winky said. "Scientists didn't call him *Allosaurus* until that particular dinosaur was extinct for millions of years."

"That's a dumb name for a dinosaur," said Slick.

"What would you have called him?" Winky asked.

"George," said Slick. "It's easier to say."

"Yes, but it doesn't sound very scientific," Winky said.

"That's what's wrong with science," said Slick. "Everything is given a name you can't pronounce, remember, or spell."

"We can argue about science class terminology once we're back in our Mystic Bay," Winky said. "We have to get back inside and charge Milo's battery if we ever hope to get out of here alive."

"How are we going to do that?" Slick asked. "I don't see any storm clouds out here, and there aren't any clouds on the horizon."

"We won't need clouds to charge the battery," Winky said. "I've come up with an alternative plan."

142

"Oh, brother."

"This is a good one," Winky said. "It came to me while I was wrapping the aluminum clothesline around our dinosaur's tooth."

"I think your brain has been affected by the bad breath fumes," said Slick.

"I'm convinced that this will work," Winky said.

"You always are," Slick said as the boys climbed down to their time machine. "What are you going to do this time?"

"I'm going to run a wire from Milo's battery down to the dinosaur's stomach juices."

"I don't think Milo's battery runs on dinosaur food," Slick said. "Besides, what are you going to use for wire? "I already used up all of my dad's train wire helping you build the time machine."

"My mother's aluminum clothesline should do the job," Winky said, and then attached it to one of the dead battery's terminals. "Cross your fingers; this might be our only chance of ever going home."

"I still don't get it," said Slick. "How is that clothesline going to help us get out of here?"

"If dipping the aluminum wire down in the dinosaur's stomach acid shocked both of us, it might do the same thing to Milo's battery," Winky said. "It's a good thing you brought all of my mother's clothesline with you. We're going to need it."

"Isn't there a faster way to charge Milo's battery?" Slick asked. "That lightning bolt back at your dad's garage did the job in less than a second."

"If you see a stray lightning bolt in here, let me know," Winky said. He went back to work setting up his makeshift prehistoric battery charger.

Once he was confident the clothesline was making contact with the dinosaur's stomach acid, Winky decided to take one last look at their swamp. Slick joined him at the *Tyrannosaurus'* teeth, and the boys gazed out on prehistoric Mystic Bay.

A golden flash caught Winky's eye.

"Hey, what's that?" He pointed down at the giant boulder below them that seemed to be shimmering in the blazing sun.

"I can't tell from up here," Slick said. "Is that the rock that the T-rex cracked open when he was chasing us?"

"I think so." Winky took out his phone to take a picture. He thought he saw something golden embedded in the stone.

Suddenly, the boys were overwhelmed by an odor that reminded them of an automobile burning. It was a metallic smell. A dense cloud of smoke filled the dinosaur's mouth.

Slick yelled, "The dinosaur is on fire!"

Winky and Slick quickly joined Scooter beside the time machine. The boys stared at the aluminum wire leading from Milo Snitzer's bus battery down to the pool of digestive acid.

The stomach acid was slowly fizzing its way up the dinosaur's throat. Their clothesline was red hot, and no longer silver in color. Smoke continued filling the inside of the dinosaur's mouth as the acid boiled.

"Quick, get back in the time machine," Winky said while he carelessly plunked Scooter down on the seat. "Our battery must be charging faster than I thought."

Afraid to touch the glowing clothesline, Winky kicked the aluminum wire free of their battery. The wire disappeared down the reptile's throat.

Milo's battery was hot, and even their wooden seat was smoking. Winky forced himself to reconnect the dangling wire. He crossed his fingers when finished and hoped that he had reattached it correctly.

While Winky tightened the connection, the lower portion of the dinosaur's jaw began to dissolve. The stomach acid began flowing into the swamp. The acid continued dissolving its way through the reptile's flesh, and anything else it touched. Then, the time machine started sliding toward the huge opening.

"We're going to fall into the swamp and drown!" Slick said.

"There's nowhere else to run; take a look," Winky said. He pointed down through the gaping hole in the dinosaur's body.

Winky was correct; there wasn't anywhere to go. A huge black hole was now where the swamp had been. The acid had dissolved the land beneath them. All the boys could see when they stared down were what appeared to be stars. The prehistoric world of the dinosaurs was dissolving before their eyes.

"I think I know why the dinosaurs disappeared from the face of the earth," Winky said.

"Why?"

"I think we dissolved them when we came here in our time machine. We destroyed their environment," Winky said. "There's nothing left of the swamp."

"I think they died because of indigestion," said Slick. "Look how strong their stomach acid is."

Another chunk of the dinosaur's jaw dropped off and passed through the black hole that once had been the swamp. The mass of teeth and flesh fell until it was absorbed by the blackness of space. Off in the distance, a white crescent glowed among the stars.

"I think we're next," Slick yelled. "Winky, do something!"

Winky panicked. Quickly, he inserted the screwdriver and shoved it forward all the way, desperately trying to move them to a different time, but nothing happened. Another chunk of dinosaur jaw fell off, launching their time machine toward the mysterious black hole.

Scooter barked a final message to Winky. He hoped Winky heard him. It would be their only hope of escaping back to their own time.

"Thanks, Scooter," Winky said. "I didn't see the other wire on the transformer come loose."

Slick held Scooter while they tumbled out of the dinosaur. Winky managed to grab the end of the wire floating inside their cockpit before he lost it. If he was lucky, he would be able to reconnect the wire to the transformer and save them.

Winky thought that there might be enough electricity stored in Milo's battery to send them to another time; and if they were lucky, home. He jammed the wire against the transformer, just before they would have dropped into the black hole and disappeared forever.

Sparks flew inside their time machine when Winky made contact with the transformer. The fan whirled to life and the boys vanished into thin air. Now, they were racing forward in time. The sun was a solid ring of fire circling the earth. Somehow, Winky had forced the screwdriver through another section of plastic.

The boys were racing back toward their Mystic Bay, gladly leaving the prehistoric version far behind them.

There was only one problem. The boys were traveling so fast that it was impossible for them to tell when they reached the exact month, day, and year they had departed from their Mystic Bay.

"Well, here goes nothing," Winky said. He yanked the wire off the transformer in order to stop their time machine. Somehow, they had to check the date.

"Where are we? Is it safe here?" Slick asked. "Can I open my eyes? Are we back in Mystic Bay?"

"We never left it," Winky said, and smiled.

Slick dared to sneak a peek at his new surroundings. First, he opened one eye, then the

147

other. Next, he held his hands up in front of his face and started shouting. Something was wrong.

"Go back, go back! Winky, we have to go back to the swamp!" Slick yelled. "Start our time machine!"

"Why?" Winky asked while he waited for his eyes to adjust. "There must be a power outage."

"I'm blind! I left my eyes back inside the dinosaur," Slick hollered and reached out to feel if he was still inside the time machine. He was.

"It's nighttime, silly. Apparently, there's no moon out tonight," Winky said. He continued scanning the horizon for a streetlight, anything that looked like the old Mystic Bay he left behind. "I don't see any lights at all. I hope we didn't damage the town's generator."

"You should have stopped when it was daylight," Slick said. "You know I'm afraid of the dark."

"Look, isn't that a campfire over there?" Winky asked. "Someone's having a party down by the bay."

"I think you're right. I can hear people. They sound like they are singing," Slick said. Both boys fell silent and strained to hear the words.

"Umm-ga, umm-ga, umm-ga, umm-ga," came drifting through the crisp night air.

The voices were distant, but sounded strangely familiar. At least they were human. It was good to hear people singing again in Mystic Bay.

"That song reminds me of the ancient tribal ceremony held out on the Bay every summer," Slick said with a sigh. "It sure is good to be home again. Finally, I feel safe. No more dinosaurs."

Scooter barked a word of caution, but as usual, the beagle did not elaborate. Slick ignored him, but Winky didn't. He sensed that the beagle was trying to warn him about some impending danger.

"What's wrong, Scooter?" Winky asked. Then he heard voices that were too close for comfort.

The people approaching were carrying torches--a lot of torches. That was unusual for Mystic Bay. Usually, the people carried flashlights at night.

A huge, prehistoric-looking man dressed only in animal skins suddenly appeared and screamed, "Umm-ga, wom-ba, wom-ba!" He thrust his torch into the ground, and then charged their time machine.

The man wielding the huge club over his head feigned an attack, and then ran back to the safety of his torch. The other cavemen watched on as their leader performed this ceremony several more times. Winky tried to start his time machine, but he had dropped the loose wire again and was unable to locate it in the darkness.

"Wom-ba, wom-ba, wom-ba!" the caveman screamed. He charged the boys again with his club raised high above his head.

"This isn't our Mystic Bay!" Slick yelled. "Get us out of here!"

---

See if you can figure out what was glimmering in the rock that the T-rex cracked open by studying Winky's photo at **www.WinkyStudmire.com**. Winky would love to hear your theories!

# CHAPTER 16
## The Original Residents of Mystic Bay

Scooter growled, and then leaped out of the boys' time machine. It was a clever maneuver on the beagle's part. He did not attack the caveman. His sole reason for growling was to buy time to escape.

Winky and Slick followed Scooter's lead, only they weren't growling at the caveman. They knew better than to provoke the shaggy creature wielding the club. "Quick, run into the woods and hide," Winky yelled as the caveman charged their time machine.

"Like I was going to stand there and greet him," Slick said under his breath as he ran.

The rest of the cavemen slowly began to surround the time machine. Had the boys not run when they did, the other cavemen would have ambushed them.

Each was armed with a club and a torch. Collectively, their torches lit up the area around the time machine.

Winky glanced back to get a better look at what was chasing him. He didn't like what he saw. Slick had been correct. The boys were not back in their Mystic Bay, not yet. They had another million years to go, more or less, before reaching their own time.

The caveman had a face that looked like it had been squeezed in a carpenter's vise. Bushy eyebrows protruded from the man's forehead. It was as though they had been designed as miniature canopies. They protected the brute's eyes from the harsh glare of the sun. His nose was broad and flat, his teeth, brown.

"That is one big dude," Winky said to Slick.

"Your dude needs some new clothes," said Slick.

"He needs a haircut and a shave," Winky said.

"I bet he has fleas," Slick added.

Coarse black hair covered the exposed areas of the caveman's body. Patches of pale skin peeked out from beneath the hair. His clothes smelled of dead animal skins that had not been cured properly. Winky itched just looking at them.

"You're probably right about the fleas," Winky whispered. "Don't move, and keep quiet."

"Wom-ba, wom-ba, wom-ba," the caveman shouted while he tried to smash the wagon into little pieces.

Winky thought it best not to converse with the man. Instead, he started running deeper into the forest and didn't look back again until he felt safe.

Finally, Winky stopped behind a large tree, and then so did Slick. Once they stopped running, the boys were able to catch their breaths and assess the situation.

Though neither boy mentioned it, both hoped the caveman hadn't destroyed their time machine. They wanted to go home. Traveling through time wasn't as much fun as each thought it would be.

"Did you see the size of the club that guy was carrying? Our time machine's toast," Winky said.

Slick looked around the massive tree to see what was happening to their wagon. "I don't think we have to worry about the time machine being trashed," he said. "When did you add the anti-theft device?"

"What are you blabbering about?" Winky asked.

"Check it out for yourself," said Slick.

Winky peeked around the large tree trunk. Their caveman repeatedly charged at the time machine with his stone-tipped club held high above his head. And every time he tried to smash the wagon, a bolt of lightning shot out from Milo's battery and nailed the club. The force of the shock stunned the caveman, but he didn't stop. Twice, he fell to the ground and stayed there for almost a minute.

"That last flash was really bright. What's happening?" Slick asked.

"That dinosaur acid is powerful stuff. Milo's battery must be fully charged," Winky said. "Our caveman is trapped in some kind of time loop that is being generated by our time machine."

"So what's our crayon man doing now?" Slick asked.

"I think you mean Cro-Magnon, don't you?" Winky said, giving Slick his best gifted-student smile.

"Cro-Magnon, that's it," Slick said. "I almost had it correct the first time. Miss Dalrymple taught us all about him last week. I think I missed that question on the test."

"Look on the bright side; you can teach her all about cavemen next week," Winky said. "I doubt if she will believe you, though."

"Why not?" Slick asked.

"Cro-Magnon remains have never been discovered in Mystic Bay," Winky said.

"Are you going to go tell our caveman that he is lost?"

"I'll pass. You can tell him if you want to." Winky continued watching the caveman battle their time machine.

The boys watched the caveman time loop until they got bored with the show. Then the unexpected happened. The Cro-Magnon's screams--and the bolts of lightning from Milo's battery--attracted the entire tribe of cavemen. They were not used to having a source of light, other than their torches, after the sun went down.

The other cavemen were terrified of the time machine when they saw how it zapped their leader. The flashes of light frightened them. They dropped their clubs, planted their torches, and got down on their knees to worship this fire god that had overpowered their chief.

"I wonder if our time machine would have the same effect on the girls back in Mystic Bay." Slick asked and pictured all of the cheerleaders chasing after him.

"I don't think so," Winky answered, snapping Slick out of his reverie.

"Well, we have to build a machine to attract girls when we return to our Mystic Bay," Slick said.

"I will work on developing the *Slickster Super Duper Girl Attractor* when we get back home," Winky said.

"Can I help you build it?" Slick asked.

"Yes, but only if we live long enough to get back to our Mystic Bay," Winky said.

Suddenly, he heard a whistling sound and roughly pushed Slick aside. "Look out, Slick!"

A spear sailed by and landed precisely where Slick had been standing. "Run!" Winky yelled. "It looks like the whole tribe is coming after us!"

Five muscular cave-women were in hot pursuit of the boys. They were not as impressed by the time machine as their men were.

"This wasn't the way I wanted to meet girls!" Slick yelled while he ran through the woods. "What did you do to make them so angry?"

"I didn't do anything, honest," Winky said when a second spear whizzed past him. He looked back over his shoulder. "Quick, duck in here! They're busy chasing Scooter."

Scooter turned, growled, and barked at the cave-women. They were not afraid of dogs and viewed him as a potential meal. A prehistoric axe almost struck his tail, but it missed. Only the wooden shaft slapped against his hindquarters.

Scooter barked for the boys to wait up for him. The beagle found himself confused by all the strange sounds and smells.

"We're over here, Scooter! Come on boy," Winky yelled while he continued running through the woods.

Winky hoped that Scooter heard him. He had no intention of going back for the beagle, not as long as those weapons were flying through the air.

"Can't you run any faster?" Slick asked.

"I'm trying," Winky said. "Head back to the time machine."

"Why? That's where the hairy caveman with the giant club is waiting for us."

"I realize that, but we have to try to escape from this time before those cave-women catch us," Winky said. He put on an extra burst of speed when he saw Scooter shoot past him. "Wait for me, Scooter!"

"Winky, watch where you're running!" Slick called out, but his warning did not reach Winky in time.

The ensuing collision was a violent one.

Scooter and Slick stopped at the time machine, but Winky ran past it and into the arms of the huge caveman. Winky had been running so fast that the collision knocked the caveman free of the time loop. Furious at being humiliated in front of his tribe, the caveman picked up his club and turned his anger on Winky.

"Get over here before he nails you," Slick yelled while both he and Scooter waited nervously inside the time machine. "The cave-women are getting closer."

"I'm trying," Winky said and ran behind a small tree to avoid being clubbed.

Slick could see the cave-women heading in his direction. The other cavemen that had been worshipping the time machine did not approach it. They feared the lightning bolts, especially after seeing the power they had over their leader. Instead of attacking the wagon, they chased after Winky.

But Winky was short and agile. He easily maneuvered his way between the swinging stone clubs to the time machine.

Just when it looked like they were about to escape, Slick screamed out another warning.

# CHAPTER 17
*Into the Future*

"Winky, that caveman is going to clobber you if you don't slide into home plate!"

Slick was blabbering into the wagon's handle as though he were a sports announcer giving the play-by-play call of a player rounding third. Afraid to move, he remained seated in his make-believe press box.

"Which caveman? There must be a thousand of them chasing me!" Winky gasped, crossed his fingers, and darted sharply to his left when Slick didn't answer.

"The one getting ready to clobber you with his club," Slick finally said, but Winky had already made his move. "That's it! Keep zigzagging."

The caveman's huge club missed Winky's shoulder by less than an inch and continued downward. It pulverized a fern when it struck the ground. Determined to pound Winky into a similar state, the caveman picked up his weapon and continued the chase. He handled the club as though it were weightless.

As he ran after Winky, the caveman toyed with his club. Winky's narrow escape was about to come to an abrupt end. Slick spotted three cavemen getting ready to ambush his pal.

"Stop running! They're waiting for you behind that giant fern," Slick called out to his pal, and then made several suggestions. "Head back this way; you can outmaneuver this guy. Pretend he is Butch Slaughter back in our Mystic Bay."

"Butch is a pussycat compared to this oaf," Winky yelled as he dodged to his left and right to avoid the many blows. "I think you should try to distract him."

"I don't think that's a good idea," said Slick. "I'm not as good at dodging cavemen as you are."

"Scooter, you can run circles around him," Winky shouted. "Guys, I could use a little help out here!"

Scooter sat up and barked one wimpy bark. The beagle was afraid to leave the wagon. The cavemen wore animal hides for clothing and were not afraid of barks or bare teeth. The little dog didn't want anything to do with them.

Scooter's lone bark did prove effective, though. The caveman chasing Winky stopped running, licked his chops, and then advanced toward the time machine. Scooter looked like an easy meal, and the little dog's hide would make a perfect hat for the coming winter months. All that remained was catching the beagle. And that shouldn't be difficult; Scooter had shorter legs than Winky.

"Thanks, Scooter," Winky said. "I owe you one."

"I hope you're proud of yourself," Slick said to Scooter. "Now he's headed our way!"

The caveman took several steps toward the wagon and suddenly stopped. He remembered what the time machine had done to him. Turning, the caveman decided to go after Winky again, even if he was a harder catch.

Winky took Slick's advice and continued zigzagging to avoid being caught. When the caveman stumbled, Winky made a beeline for the wagon. Once he was safely inside the time machine, Slick tapped him on the shoulder. Winky turned and Slick handed him the wire he had disconnected earlier.

"Thanks," Winky said. "He almost grabbed me."

"You can tell me all about it later. Get us out of here," Slick said as calmly as possible. Even Scooter was quiet.

A giant *thud* broke the silence. A crudely-made axe suddenly joined the time travelers in their wagon. Luckily, the cave-woman who threw it had terrible aim, and the boys and Scooter remained unscathed.

Without uttering another word, Winky jammed the wire against the battery terminal and switched on the time machine's fan. The transformer was already set for the future. Milo's battery still had some life left in it.

How much life, the boys didn't know.

The boys tried to relax by closing their eyes. After several seconds of doing nothing, Winky decided to sneak a peek to see if there were any cavemen trapped in another time loop. There weren't, but something else was. Just inches above his head, was one of the cavemen's clubs, embedded into their protective canopy.

The caveman was gone, trapped in his own time. His club, however, along with the prehistoric axe, was now being carried forward into the future. The weapon had almost made contact with Winky's head when he activated the time machine's protective canopy. Since the time machine's canopy was invisible, the club appeared to be suspended in space.

"I hope we don't meet up with any more cavemen on the trip back to our Mystic Bay," Winky said as he stared at the huge club. "Look how close that thing came to hitting me."

"I bet these prehistoric weapons will be worth a ton of extra credit points in science class," Slick said. He reached out to grab the club above Winky's head.

"I don't think you should touch it," Winky said as the boys continued racing into the future. "What if that club sucks you back into the past?"

"Easy for you to say," Slick said. "You're passing science." He extended his hand toward the club again.

"I hope we don't lose you," Winky said.

The wooden handle and the strips of animal hide that made up part of the caveman's club turned to dust the instant Slick touched it. Only the polished rock that had been attached to the end of the club remained intact. It hovered there, inside their time machine, and refused to budge despite Slick's tugging on it.

"What happened to the rest of my club?" Slick asked while he tugged on the remaining stone.

"I'm not certain but I think your wooden club has aged a few million years in the last second or two. We are heading into the future at a fantastic speed. I hope we don't overshoot our Mystic Bay," Winky said. He decided to snap a picture of the axe before it vanished, too.

"The rock was part of the club, so why didn't it disappear?" Slick asked. He tried to pull the stone out of the air before it fell on Winky's head.

Winky, seeing why Slick was pulling on the rock, decided to scoot forward a few inches, just in case it did fall. Now that he felt safe, he thought about Slick's question before answering. Winky smiled when he came up with an answer that made sense.

"Rocks age much slower than living things," Winky said. "If I were you, I would keep a close eye on that rock, and be careful not to touch it."

"Why?" Slick asked. "It's just a rock. Don't worry; I'll catch it if it falls."

Scooter tried to answer Slick's question, but Slick gave him one of his puzzled looks. He couldn't understand Scooter's beagle barks, and they were being amplified by the time machine's invisible canopy. Slick finally tried to quiet the little beagle.

"I wasn't talking to you," Slick said. "No more barking until we are on Winky's back porch."

Turning his back to Slick, Scooter barked, just because he could. The little beagle liked the powerful sound his barks made inside the time machine. It made him feel like a German shepherd, big and tough. That feeling quickly disappeared when Winky gave him a glaring look, followed by a warning.

"Scooter, it's time for you to be quiet," Winky said. "Your barking is getting on my nerves."

Everything outside their time machine was reduced to a blur.

"What's happening?" Slick yelled. He pointed skyward. "Did we go to Saturn? Those look like rings to me."

The sun and moon appeared as two solid bands of matter circling the planet. Now, Winky's time machine was racing faster than ever. Milo's battery had released an unexpected burst of energy.

"Those aren't rings," Winky said.

"They sure look like rings to me," said Slick.

"It's the same old thing: the sun is chasing the moon," Winky said, as he stared up, not at the rings, but deeper into outer space. "I wonder if there is another Winky out there playing with his wagon?"

Scooter barked his opinion, and Slick laughed.

"I agree, Scooter," Slick said. "One Winky per universe is more than enough."

It was impossible to estimate the year or even the century. Their time machine was racing out of control. The blur outside their canopy turned into long strands of time. Slick was the first to speak.

"Do you think it would be safe to stop and see where we are?" Slick dared ask after a short period of silence.

"Not yet. I'm going to let the time machine run a while," Winky said. "I'm worried about our battery, and I want to meet civilized people when it dies on us."

"Well, I think we should stop," Slick argued.

"I don't want to risk meeting up with anymore dinosaurs or prehistoric cavemen armed with clubs," Winky explained. "I want to smell fresh smog, hear noisy automobiles, and see men armed with briefcases when we make our next stop; that I can handle."

"I hate it when you make sense. Keep going," Slick said. He fell silent while he stared at the rock that was still suspended inside their tiny cockpit.

Scooter was now watching it, too. Something was wrong. Winky saw Scooter and looked up at the rock. It was crumbling. Beneath it was a small pile of what appeared to be dust on their seat. The rock was shrinking in size. Like an hourglass, the rock was now recording the passing of time as it continued to shed fine grains of what looked to be sand.

"Stop our time machine!" Slick shouted. "The rock is coming apart. We might be next!"

"I don't think that can happen, but I'm not certain," Winky said. He reached down and pulled off one of the red wires on the transformer.

Time again stopped on Mystic Bay, a different Mystic Bay than they had ever seen before. There was no mistaking that familiar shoreline. The sand was gone, but the land gently curved and disappeared off to their right into the ocean.

"Well, we're home. At least I guess it's home," Winky said.

"It looks like a giant fishbowl resting on black sand," Slick said. He stared out at the dark glass bubble standing next to their time machine. "What happened to your house, and where's the driveway?"

"I don't know," Winky said. "Everything's changed since we left. This isn't my backyard."

Scooter barked in pain. A high-pitched whining sound hurt the beagle's ears. An object suddenly shot past them, refusing to be trapped in time. The boys watched, both fascinated and frightened at the same time.

This wasn't the past.

The rocket-mobile raced across the landscape in a haphazard manner. It darted about like a dragonfly, starting and stopping without any warning. And it didn't touch the ground, even when it came to a stop. It hovered.

Slick was the first to speak.

"I'll bet that's my mom looking for me," Slick said. "She drives like that when she's angry."

"I don't think that's her," Winky said. He silently wondered if they would ever find their way home. "I don't know if I like this Mystic Bay. We've gone too far into the future. I think we're lost. Again."

This Mystic Bay had no roads, trees, or any plant life. There was lush foliage growing inside the glass bubbles. The spheres had replaced the houses on Winky's street, and each one was identical. Mystic Bay now resembled sketches of what a space colony on Mars might look like, if humans ever settled there.

And the sky was black--not blue--even though the sun burned high above them. Stars were visible, too. It was both beautiful and scary at the same time. Winky wondered how far into the future they had traveled. He preferred his Mystic Bay to this one.

"I can't feel any heat from the sun," said Slick.

"I think we overshot our year," Winky said while he studied this alien-looking settlement. "At least there aren't any dinosaurs or cavemen chasing us."

"Even the plants are dead around here. What could have killed off all of our trees?" Slick asked.

"Probably the ultraviolet rays from the sun wiped them out," Winky said. "It looks like earth has lost most of its atmosphere. I wonder where it went."

"How can you tell that it's missing?" Slick asked. "I thought air was supposed to be invisible."

"We had blue skies with white clouds floating about, except when a storm rolled in, remember?" Winky asked, answering Slick's question with another.

"Sure, and the bay was blue, too," Slick said.

"That's because it was the sky that made the bay appear blue," Winky explained as he stared up at the blackness that hovered ominously over this Mystic Bay.

"I didn't know that," said Slick. "I always wondered why the bay was blue."

There was a brief pause in their conversation as both boys stared out at the ocean. The waves sounded familiar, but its black color reminded them of the prehistoric swamp where the dinosaurs attacked them.

"What do you think of this Mystic Bay?" Winky asked.

"I don't like the future," Slick answered. "I sure hope you can find the reverse gear on our time machine. I want to go back to our Mystic Bay."

"Me, too," Winky said. He adjusted the screwdriver's setting before reconnecting the red wire to the transformer. "There, that should do it. Next stop, home… I hope."

"What did you do to our time machine?" Slick asked.

"I reversed a couple wires on your transformer before reattaching the red one," Winky said. "And I also reduced the speed setting so we can see what's happening outside. Blurs are boring to watch."

"I hope this won't take long," Slick said. "I haven't eaten a thing since we left your garage."

"It shouldn't take more than a million years to get back home," Winky said, and Slick fell silent.

The boys started going back in time, slowly at first. Winky gradually increased the speed until time was passing at what he assumed to be the rate of one year per minute. Then, he increased it to one year per second.

Winky was merely guessing as to how fast time was actually passing outside their wagon. There were no gauges for measuring the passage of time on board their time machine. That was something Winky planned on correcting if he ever built another model.

"How much longer?" Slick finally asked when his stomach started growling. "Are we almost home?"

"No, and don't ask me again. I'll tell you when we get there," Winky blurted out, suddenly sounding like his father on one of their summer vacations.

"This is worse than traveling to Florida with my parents," Slick said. "We're lost, aren't we?"

"We are not lost. This is Mystic Bay. Everything is going to be just like it was, I promise," Winky said, trying to reassure his pal. "All we have to do is stop our time machine on the exact date that we left."

"That's easy," Slick said. "Just check your phone."

"I already tried that," Winky said. "It keeps displaying the time we left Mystic Bay. I can't figure out why."

"Well, what about my new calendar watch? It shows the month, day, and the year. Phooey, Milo's battery magnetized it. It's running backwards."

"You mean that you had that watch all this time and didn't say anything?" Winky said.

"I forgot that I had it in my pocket," Slick said. This revelation brought Scooter out of his pouting mode. He barked angrily at Slick for being so forgetful. The beagle couldn't wait to get home. He was in the mood to chase some neighborhood cats. His leg muscles were getting stiff in the cramped quarters of the time machine.

"So what is today's date?" Winky asked.

"I don't know; I accidentally hit a button and the screen went blank. I just got this watch last week from my aunt," Slick said, clearly embarrassed that he did not have the slightest idea as to which button to push to get the date on the display screen.

"Your minute is up. What's the date?" Winky asked. "We need the correct date!"

"I know that you have to push one of these buttons," Slick said as he jabbed frantically at the maze of buttons on his watch. Nothing happened.

Scooter barked and brushed Slick's hand aside. Next, he pressed his nose on the first button and the tiny screen displayed the month, the day, and the year. Slick just sat there with his mouth open.

"Good boy, Scooter," Winky said and scratched the beagle behind his ears. "Slick, you're hopeless."

"Lucky guess," Slick said. He studied his watch. "It's Saturday, the 1st, no, make that Thursday, the 20th, wait, stop the time machine so I can read this display. We're traveling too fast for me to get an accurate reading."

Winky removed the red wire on the transformer. They were home. A familiar-looking Mystic Bay stood before them. Winky's house was right where it should be, and so was the driveway. But there was still something wrong.

Something was different about it.

The automobile parked in the driveway was small and efficient looking, nothing like the used clunkers his father usually drove. And Winky's house was a different color, a yellow instead of the usual dull beige. And two old people were now living in his parents' house. He could see them through the window.

"Slick, what's the date?" Winky asked.

"Saturday, the 27th," Slick answered.

"No, what is the year?" Winky repeated. "I need to know what year this is."

"This can't be right. But it's what the screen says, honest," Slick said, shrugging his shoulders and shoving his watch into Winky's field of vision.

Winky barely registered what Slick was showing him. He just sat there, watching the old couple inside his house. A copy of the *Mystic Times* was on the back porch. Fred Studmire, Winky's father, always had his newspaper delivered to the back door.

"Those are my parents," Winky said. He didn't want to believe what he was seeing.

"That can't be your parents," said Slick. "Those are old people living in your house."

Winky got out of the time machine and walked over to his steps. He was tempted to knock on the door. Instead, he reached down for the paper.

The newspaper was cool to the touch, and very smooth. It was not made out of paper.

"Slick, look, they're printing the *Times* on plastic instead of paper," Winky said.

"Get out of here," said Slick.

"It's true, honest," Winky said. "Come over here and look for yourself if you don't believe me."

Slick got out of the wagon and ambled his way over to where Winky was standing. He bent over and touched the paper while Winky glanced down at the date.

"Check out the date," Winky said, and Slick did as he was told.

It was printed in small print just above the headline.

The boys were only forty years late for supper.

---

To see Winky's amazing photos from the distant past and future, go to **www.WinkyStudmire.com**. Be sure to tease Slick about his new prehistoric girlfriend while you're there!

## CHAPTER 18
*Frozen for Good*

"That has to be a pretend copy of the *Mystic Times*," Slick argued. "They don't make newspapers out of plastic."

"Well, they will in the future," Winky said. He stepped away from the newspaper on his back porch.

"How can you be so sure about that?" Slick asked.

"Because we are in the future," Winky said.

Winky started walking back to their time machine, stopped, and then turned. He studied his house for the longest time. Winky found himself staring at the old couple seated by the kitchen window. They looked strangely familiar, but he didn't want to recognize them. But deep down, he knew they were his parents.

"You're thinking again," Slick said. "I can tell by that look on your face. What's the problem?"

"We are still in the future. I've got to get us back home," Winky said. He boarded the time machine, and gently pulled back on the screwdriver.

"Aren't you supposed to push on the screwdriver?" Slick asked as the attic fan came to life.

"Not on this trip," Winky answered.

"Why?" Slick asked in his usual annoying manner.

"I want to go home," Winky said. "Cross your fingers. I hope we don't lose control of the fan."

Winky kept an eye on the world outside their time machine. The boys continued traveling back through time. At least, Winky thought they were. It was impossible to tell for certain.

Nothing appeared to be changing in Mystic Bay. Actually, it was happening too fast for the boys to detect. Suddenly, without any warning, the futuristic glass bubble houses reappeared on the block where Winky lived. "Milo's dumb battery must have reversed its electron flow," Winky said.

"Are you sure about that?" Slick asked.

"No, but take a peek outside," Winky said, and then quickly grabbed the screwdriver and pushed it forward until a blue sky once again lit up their protective canopy. "We were going the wrong way."

"How could the battery do that?" Slick asked.

"Beats me," Winky said. "I hope it has enough electrons stored inside to get us back to our Mystic Bay. I'm tired of these surprises."

"Me, too," Slick said and glanced at his watch.

The boys were once again traveling back in time. Winky sensed that they were closing in on their year. Staring out at the countryside made both Slick and Winky dizzy.

Suddenly, the sun came to an abrupt halt directly overhead. It baked him, just like when he was at the beach. Milo's battery had died again, but not before it had powered him back to their Mystic Bay, or so Winky believed.

"You did it! We're back home," Slick said after he checked the backyard for any dinosaur tracks. "I didn't think you would ever find our Mystic Bay."

"Neither did I," Winky said. He joined Slick out in the backyard for a brisk walk.

Scooter reluctantly abandoned the wagon and joined the boys. He thought it best to stay close, just in case a dinosaur or a caveman followed him through time. It felt good to stretch his hind legs after all the time he spent in Winky's tiny wagon.

"It's great to be home," said Slick. "I wonder what my mother is cooking for supper. I'm starving."

Winky checked out his backyard, his house, and his street. He quickly realized that he was going to have to give Slick more bad news. They were close to their departure time, but there was a slight problem.

"Something is wrong here," Winky said. "It wasn't like this when we left our Mystic Bay."

"What's wrong now?"

"Nothing is moving." Winky pointed up at the sky. "Look, the sea gulls and that plane are hanging motionless in the sky, just like that *Pterodactyl* in the swamp."

"A head wind could cause that," Slick said.

Slick didn't want to believe Winky and searched for any hint of movement in this Mystic Bay. Objects on land resembled statues. Everything was frozen in time, even the waves out on the bay.

"What did you do to our town?" Slick finally asked. "This place is just like the swamp."

"I think Milo's battery died before we made it back home," Winky said.

"Maybe we went back too far. We need to check the date," Slick said.

Winky headed toward the back porch and reached down for the paper. The newspaper moved, but in slow motion. It didn't matter how hard Winky pulled on the paper, it barely budged. To Slick, Winky's battle with the newspaper resembled an underwater ballet.

"How are you doing that?" Slick asked while he stretched his muscles. "I can't move that slow."

"Some objects aren't frozen in time, but they resist being moved. We must be getting closer to our original starting date," Winky said. "That's good."

"If you say so," Slick said, even though he didn't understand the concept of time as Winky explained it.

Winky felt relieved when he noticed that everything was just the way it was supposed to be around his house. Other than that, most of the loose items in the yard appeared to be still locked in time.

Winky examined the front page of the *Mystic Times*. It was filled with the usual boring news.

"How close are we?" Slick asked, and decided that it might be a good idea to stay on wagon. It never occurred to him to glance down at his watch.

Slick knew all too well how unpredictable Milo's battery could be. He did not want their time machine to leave without him. Slick figured that if the attic fan began to rotate, sitting on the wagon would enable him to stop it in time to rescue Winky.

"We are almost there," Winky eventually answered, and then decided to glance through the *Mystic Times* to see if anything exciting had happened during their absence. "Slick, this issue isn't made out of plastic, just plain old paper; that's good sign."

"Whatever," Slick said, impatiently.

Mystic Bay was a quiet little town and rarely had anything exciting to report. Winky didn't think much when he read the headline stating that no one had won yesterday's record-setting state lottery. It was a jackpot of over two hundred million dollars. The winning lottery numbers appeared directly below the headline boxed in dark print: 2,4,6,8,10, and 40.

Winky smiled when he noticed the date on the paper; it was three days in the future. The lottery money could be his for the taking, except that kids were not permitted to play the state lottery. If only Winky could convince his parents to play for him..

"Well? How close are we to getting home?" Slick asked. "What are you doing, memorizing the paper?"

"Just part of it. We are within three days of getting home," Winky said. "Quick, slide back in the seat before I forget the winning numbers. Trust me on this one. We are about to become multi-millionaires."

"Right, and I'm going to get straight A's on my next report card," Slick said.

"Have I ever let you down?" Winky asked.

"Constantly. Would you like the complete list, or just a couple examples?" Slick slid to the rear of their time machine, and waited for Winky to join him. Scooter was sitting in front of Slick. When Winky climbed on the wagon, he gave Scooter's ears a quick massage, and then reached down for the screwdriver.

This time Winky remembered how Milo's battery sometimes reversed itself. He didn't know why, only that it had happened. Pushing the screwdriver forward ever so slightly, he waited for time to start moving backwards again. This time, the sun remained locked high in the sky. Their time machine wouldn't start.

Scooter barked, trying to remind the boys that Milo's battery was dead, but neither boy was paying any attention to him. They were trapped in the wrong Mystic Bay, and Winky wanted that lottery ticket.

"Not now, Scooter," Winky said while he worked the screwdriver forward, then pulled backwards. "I'm trying to start our time machine." No matter what he tried, nothing worked.

"What seems to be the problem?" Slick asked. "I thought we were going home."

"So did I. It's the same old story," Winky said. "Our battery died." He switched into planning mode again. "Pick out a car with a good battery while I grab some tools in my dad's garage."

"Are you going to steal a battery?" Slick asked.

"No, we are just going to borrow one," Winky said. He disappeared inside the garage.

Slick checked out the cars on the street. "Winky, I found some batteries you can borrow."

"That's great," Winky said. He walked out of the garage dragging a gargantuan wrench behind him.

The wrench refused to move as fast as Winky. Winky was glad that he watched his father change the battery in their old clunker when it died last winter. Now, he had a rough idea of how to remove a battery from a car. Connecting it to the time machine would be easy; he had already done that with Milo's battery.

Winky spotted Slick standing on the sidewalk in front of his house. "Which car?" he asked.

"Take your pick," Slick said with a grin as Winky came walking down the driveway. "Why are you walking so slowly? Are you getting trapped in time?"

"No, it's this stupid wrench. It seems to have a mind of its own. I can barely move it." Winky walked over to the nearest car, a red Chevrolet with its windows down. "Slick, reach inside and pull the hood release. I'll take it from there."

"I can do that," Slick said. He leaned through the car's open window. "Winky, I was wrong; I can't do it."

"Why not?" Winky asked. "The windows are down."

"It's the hood release; the latch must be frozen in time," Slick said. The boys tried every car hood on the block without any success.

Battery after battery remained locked in time, safe from the boys. None of the car hoods would open. Neither would the car doors, and most weren't even locked. Their chances of escaping from this Mystic Bay were growing slimmer by the second.

Abandoning the parked automobiles, the boys headed down to Elmer's gas station located on Birdseed Drive. It was near the bay. There, fifty batteries greeted them when the boys turned the corner.

The batteries were neatly arranged, stacked like a small pyramid in front of the gas station. Each remained locked in time, except for the top battery. It moved slightly when Slick tried to pick it up.

"The top one is loose," Slick called out.

"I wonder why it moved and the other batteries didn't," Winky said.

He had no idea that the fan blades on their time machine had turned slightly, just as Slick tried to pick up the top battery. Winky had forgotten to remove the red power wire from the transformer.

"Who cares?" Slick asked. "We've got ourselves a battery, and a new one to boot. Let's take it back to the time machine and get out of here."

"Wait, we have to see if the battery has any electricity inside it," Winky said. "I'll get a long screwdriver from inside the gas station."

"What good is that going to do?" Slick asked.

"If we touch both terminals and get a spark, the battery has electricity inside it," Winky said.

"You must study day and night to know all this," Slick said, amazed at Winky's knowledge of electricity and car batteries. "Me, I need my sleep."

It never occurred to Slick that his pal could be mistaken. Winky disappeared inside the gas station and returned with a giant screwdriver. It had to be at least two feet long and kept hitting Winky on the ankle while he walked.

"That has to be the longest screwdriver in the world," Slick said as he stared at the tool. "Let me hold it for a second; I want to see how heavy it is."

"Here, see if you can get it to move any faster. And while you are holding it, check our battery," Winky said. He handed the screwdriver to Slick.

Slick placed their new battery down on the pavement and took the screwdriver from Winky. Squinting so that no sparks would jump into his eyes, he touched both terminals with the screwdriver, fully expecting to be electrocuted in the process. Nothing happened. Elmer's battery was dead, too.

"Rats," Winky said and kicked the battery. "All the electricity in Mystic Bay is frozen in time."

"You mean that we'll be stuck in this day for the rest of our lives?" Slick asked, panic creeping into his voice.

"It looks like you're never going to be sixteen. You can forget about driving your dad's truck," Winky answered. "And me, I'm always going to be short."

"You and your dumb inventions," Slick said and headed down to the pier. "Thanks a lot, Winky."

Winky understood Slick's frustration with their time machine and let him go on alone. While Slick walked down to the pier to be by himself, Winky managed to put everything in the store back in its proper place.

The time machine's blades were barely moving. They rotated just enough to free many of the smaller objects in town. These items would again be frozen in time the moment Milo's battery ran out of power. Each time that happened, the battery took longer to build up another charge. And each new charge was weaker than the one before.

Winky never made the connection between the battery, the fan, and the movable objects he found at the gas station. He had forgotten that the red power wire was still attached to the transformer. Had Winky remembered, he would have run back to his time machine and disconnected the wire. But that never happened.

Once he had Elmer's gas station back the way he found it, Winky hiked down to the shore to be with his pal. Both boys were trapped in time. Winky knew that they needed each other's company now more than ever.

Scooter cautiously tagged along behind Winky. He was on the lookout for predators when he thought he heard something. Growling and barking, Scooter tried to warn Winky.

Something was stalking them.

# CHAPTER 19
*Betsy to the Rescue*

"Scooter, why can't you be quiet for a change? There's nothing moving out there, and I don't hear anything. You've been jumpy ever since we stopped here," Winky said. He then turned his attention toward his other pal. "Slick, are you still mad?"

"No, but I don't think that I will ever get used to seeing the sun hanging up there day and night like a picture on a wall," Slick said. He yawned and checked the sky one more time to see if the sun had moved. It hadn't. "How are we going to know when to sleep?"

"Who cares?" Winky asked. "Now, we can stay up for as long as we want. And we don't have to get up until we feel like getting up. What time is it?"

"I'll bet it's after midnight, and we don't even know it. My watch is stuck on the date setting," Slick said. "I can hardly keep my eyes open." He yawned again and blinked his eyes. "I really miss the sound of the big waves crashing onto the rocks, and the cars honking their horns, and my mom yelling at me."

"Me, too," Winky said. He leaned heavily against the pier's railing. "I'm going to close my eyes for a second or two. My eyelids feel like sandpaper."

"That sounds like a good idea," said Slick.

The boys dozed out on the pier. Scooter went back to their time machine. He preferred snoozing on the time machine's soft seat. There was something different about this Mystic Bay--no fishy smells over by the pier. Other than the boys, there wasn't anything to sniff. Even the shrubs were odor free. He barked at his favorite tree and startled the boys.

"It's only Scooter," a yawning Slick said.

Winky sat up. "It's boring around here with everything frozen in time. There is nothing to do, no one else to play with, no girls to tease. I prefer going to school to this."

"I'm not *that* bored. I like not going to school," Slick said. He fought to keep his eyes open. "I guess our parents won't be yelling at us anymore."

"I already miss my mother telling me to clean up my room," Winky said.

Scooter joined them and yelled at the boys again, but to Slick, it was just a series of annoying barks. He shrugged his shoulders and smiled at the beagle. Then, he bent down and gave the dog a halfhearted hug.

"Thanks, Scooter," Slick said. "I hope you're not offended, but it just isn't the same coming from you. I miss my mom. I want to go home."

Scooter nodded that he understood and stopped barking. Sometimes it was better to be quiet. It wasn't like Slick to miss his parents.

Winky stood up. "Let's see if we can figure a way out of here and get back to our Mystic Bay."

Scooter barked excitedly at the prospect of entering a Mystic Bay filled with familiar smells. The beagle ran down to the end of the pier and back while Winky stood next to Slick. Slick just stood there while Winky tried to come up with an escape plan.

The boys left the pier and headed toward a nearby park. A sound coming from the parking lot across the street caught Winky's attention. Then, he spotted the object that Scooter tried to warn them about.

An old orange tractor was chugging away with its lights on. That could only mean one thing: electricity.

"I know that tractor," Winky said while the boys raced over to the park for a closer look. "Wow, everything is starting to move."

Back at their time machine, the fan blades began rotating ever so slowly, just enough to cause a hint of life to come back to the tractor's battery. Sea gulls once again flew above the town, but only at a snail's pace. You had to look closely to detect any movement in their wings. The boys were more concerned with the orange tractor, especially its battery.

"That's 'Betsy,' Verne Randolph's old tractor," Slick said when they finally reached the parking lot.

"You're right," Winky said. "There's only one tractor in town like that. I hope that tractor battery has enough power to get us back to our Mystic Bay." He tried to figure out where the battery was on the tractor. It wasn't under the seat.

"I found it!" Slick yelled. "It's up front."

"Good, let's take Verne's battery back to our time machine and get out of here," Winky said. "You take one cable, and I'll grab the other. Together, we'll disconnect the battery at the same time."

"Okay," Slick said. "You take the black one; I've got the red one. Let's do it before we chicken out."

Winky and Slick each grabbed hold of a cable, said a prayer that they wouldn't get electrocuted, and then yanked as hard as they could. The battery cables slipped off, effortlessly.

The electricity stored in Verne's tractor battery didn't zap Winky or Slick when they grabbed the worn cables. Grease had oozed from the battery poles onto the old wires and provided the necessary insulation. It was so typical of Verne; he always used too much grease whenever he lubricated anything on his tractor.

Why Verne's battery still had power still puzzled the boys, especially since all of the other batteries in town were dead. But, had they gone back and checked on them, the boys would have found them fully charged. Their new world suddenly sprang to life.

Fate was offering them another brief opportunity to escape.

Back at their time machine, the fan's blades were already freewheeling. Time was once again beginning to slow again in this Mystic Bay. The charge that had built up in Milo's battery had been consumed by Winky's fan. But as long as the fan's blades continued rotating, Verne's battery would be charged.

It was not the time for dilly-dallying.

Winky and Slick took turns carrying Verne's battery back to their time machine. It was almost too heavy for either boy as they grunted their way up the street. After traipsing up the street for what seemed like hours, the boys finally reached their goal.

"Quick, connect Verne's battery to our time machine; I'll hold it in my lap," Slick said. "I can't wait to go home. I sure hope its suppertime."

"First, we have to make one more stop back in time," Winky said as he touched the clothesline to the battery. Sparks flew, and the time machine vanished.

"I knew you were going to pull a stunt like this," Slick said as the fan blades whirled. "I don't want to go back in time anymore. We could end up in that dinosaur swamp, or worse."

Scooter agreed with Slick and tried to squeeze in between Winky and the train transformer, but the space was too small for the beagle. A tail accidentally struck Winky's makeshift throttle.

Their trip back in time took an unexpected detour.

It really wasn't Scooter's fault. The time machine's cockpit was designed to hold two boys-- not two boys, a beagle, and Verne's huge tractor battery.

Safely inside their protective canopy, the world outside was nothing more than a blur. The familiar looking Mystic Bay was gone, but neither boy noticed that until Winky regained control. A rocket ship was high above this futuristic Mystic Bay. Winky couldn't tell if the ship was landing or taking off.

This rocket froze in time when Winky removed a wire from the tractor battery. Unlike Milo's battery, Verne's battery had the power to stopped time in the distant future. Winky made a mental note of this phenomenon in case he ever decided to build another time machine.

"I'm going to have permanent dents on my thighs from holding this thing," Slick said as he balanced Verne's tractor battery on his lap. "How much longer do I have to hold on to it?"

"Just a couple hundred more years. Now sit still," Winky said.

Winky had no idea of when he should stop their time machine, even though he had Slick's watch to give him the date. Time was passing by too quickly for it to be of any use. All he could do was make an educated guess based on subtle changes in his backyard. Winky knew they were running out of power. One more mistake on his part could prove disastrous.

Every now and then, Winky would risk removing one of the wires from the battery terminals. When time once again stopped, he would check the date on the newspaper on his back porch. Slick would take that opportunity to shove Verne's tractor battery down on Winky's seat and give his legs a much-needed rest.

The closer they got to their own time, the more movement there was in Mystic Bay. Winky was the first to notice this when he stopped to check the date on his father's paper. On one stop, he looked up and saw a single engine plane towing a huge red banner.

The banner invited everyone in Mystic Bay to an open house at Baxter's construction site. Winky smiled when he noticed the date was just 2 days in the future, and he decided to get out of the time machine. So did Scooter. Slick wasn't sure what was going on and remained seated.

"Where are you going? Are we home?" Slick asked, and then glanced down at his watch. "Winky, it's the wrong day."

"I know; everything is going exactly as I planned," Winky said. He started walking toward town.

"Winky, look, your mother is moving. Hello, Mrs. Studmire. Mrs. Studmire, it's me," Slick said when he got out of the time machine. "Hey, something's wrong here. Your mother can't see or hear us. Are we dead?"

"No, and you're not a ghost. I told you that we have to make one more stop before we can go back to our time," Winky said. He waved to his mother. "What are we having for supper? Mom, can you hear me?"

Linda Studmire didn't see or hear anything over by the large oak tree. She continued into the house carrying her laundry basket. Her phone was ringing.

"You were right, Slick. She didn't see me wave," Winky said. He dropped his hand down by his side.

"I don't like this," Slick said. "We should get out of here and go back to our time right now."

"Trust me, this is our last stop before we go back to our Mystic Bay," Winky said. He continued walking through a Mystic Bay that wouldn't exist for another two days. "Being invisible is kind of neat."

"I hope this is only temporary," Slick said.

"It is," said Winky in a voice that was none too confident.

"Exactly where are we going?" Slick asked.

"To *Dingledorf's Newsstand* to buy one winning lottery ticket," Winky said. He checked his pockets. "I need fifty cents. How much money do you have?"

"Two dimes and a nickel," Slick answered. "What do you want with just one lousy lottery ticket? My dad buys them by the handful, and he still hasn't won."

Winky smiled but said nothing to give his plan away to Slick. He only had one more problem to solve before reaching *Dingledorf's*. Winky had to find another quarter in order to buy his lottery ticket.

"There it is!" Winky shouted, causing Slick to bolt into the nearest open doorway and hide. He was still jumpy after their run-ins with the dinosaurs and the cavemen.

"That's the quarter we needed," Winky said. He stooped over and picked up the soda pop bottle.

"Winky, are you feeling all right?" Slick asked as he came out of hiding.

"Sure, why?" Winky asked. "Is something wrong?"

"That's a plastic bottle you're holding, not a quarter," Slick answered. "Maybe you should stop and take a quick nap. I think you have lotto fever."

"Trust me; thanks to Mr. Dingledorf's recycling efforts, this is as good as any quarter. Give me your twenty-five cents and I will make you a multi-millionaire," Winky said. He held out his hand.

"Sure, you will," Slick said, but he reluctantly gave his pal all the money he had in his pockets.

The boys walked down Main Street and entered *Dingledorf's*. As usual, no one was working the lottery counter. Winky struck the customer bell next to the lottery machine, but it wouldn't ring.

That's when Winky decided to take matters into his own hands. "Winky, you're not supposed to go behind the counter unless you work here," Slick said.

"Don't worry. I'm not going to take anything without paying for it."

"I guess Mr. Dingledorf won't mind, as long as you pay for whatever you take," said Slick.

"That's why I borrowed your twenty-five cents," He walked over to the lottery machine.

Reading the instructions on how to operate the lottery buttons, Winky punched in the numbers 2, 4, 6, 8, 10, and 40. Next, he hit the "Enter" key, but nothing happened. As far as this Mystic Bay was concerned, the boys did not exist.

"Rats, nothing works here," Winky said and hit the side of the lottery machine as hard as he could.

*Ding.*

A single lottery ticket popped up and the cash register opened. Winky took the winning ticket and placed two quarters, two dimes, a nickel, and the pop bottle on the open drawer to cover the cost of the ticket. Slick was satisfied with the transaction.

Without stopping to check his numbers, Winky jammed the lottery ticket into his front pocket. Next, the boys ran back to their time machine as fast as they could. Scooter trotted along behind them.

"We have to reset the controls so that we move very slowly in time," Winky said as he carefully adjusted the screwdriver wedged in the transformer.

"What do you want me to do?" Slick asked.

"Keep an eye on your watch's date display," Winky said as he continued checking their time machine for any loose wires or incorrect settings.

"I can do that," Slick said. "But why do we have to go so slow?" Slick asked. "I want to get home as fast as possible."

"We only have to move backward in time for a day or so," Winky said. "Actually, you can forget about your watch; I have a better idea."

"What's that?"

"Let me know the second you spot Elgin Fremont's patrol boat," said Winky.

"What if he's on the other side of the bay?" Slick asked. "How am I ever going to see him?"

"Elgin was on this side of the bay when we left my backyard. I remember hearing him tooting his foghorn during the storm." Winky made some final adjustments to the wiring. "I hope Verne's battery doesn't die on us. Cross your fingers. Here we go!"

## CHAPTER 20
*Home*

Under the watchful eyes of Slick and Scooter, Winky stopped and started the time machine a total of fifty-seven times. After making all those stops, he still had not successfully completed his mission. Traveling to the exact second of their departure was turning out to be quite a challenge.

To make matters worse, Verne's tractor battery was almost dead from Winky's efforts. Sparks no longer shot out from the rotating fan blades. Their time machine was running out of juice. It looked like the boys might not make it back to their Mystic Bay. Minutes--no, seconds--separated them from home.

"Stop, I mean go forward, no, back up." Slick kept yelling when he thought that he spotted Elgin's patrol boat out on the bay. "Well, it looked like Elgin's boat. Keep going. Winky, stop our time machine, *now*."

Scooter barked, relaying each of Slick's commands to Winky. The beagle was driving both boys crazy. Everyone's tempers were strained. Winky had to fight the urge to give up and hike down to the bay.

"I heard Slick the first time," Winky said, and then removed a wire from Verne's tractor battery.

"See? Winky knows what I mean. Don't worry about it, Scooter," Slick said. "Winky, I meant go back in time, not stop. Time travel is very confusing."

Scooter barked and shook his head in disgust. They were getting nowhere fast. Soon, they wouldn't be going anywhere, not at the rate they were draining Verne's battery. Winky started back in time, again.

"Stop," Slick said. He pointed down to the bay.

"This time it better be Elgin's boat," Winky said. "I'm going to smash that watch of yours if you don't stop looking at it instead of the bay."

"We don't have the greatest view from your backyard," Slick said, defending his actions.

"I never realized that there were so many boats like Elgin's out on the bay," Winky said.

Scooter agreed with his pal, and then tried to escape from the time machine when he spotted Mr. Dillon's cat. The little beagle never did figure out the secret of the invisible canopy. Scooter kept bumping into it every time Mr. Dillon's cat, Crissy, stuck her nose in Winky's backyard.

Suddenly, the time machine stopped. Scooter escaped, and so did Crissy. The last the boys saw the pair was when they zoomed around the front of Winky's house and raced up the street.

"I'm glad that Scooter is bugging Crissy instead of us for a change," Slick said as he shoved Verne's battery into the space previously occupied the beagle.

"Me, too." He stretched. "I think we're finally back in my backyard." He quickly got out of the time machine before it took off again for some other Mystic Bay. "For a while there, I was convinced that we were going to spend our lives trapped in the past."

"Not me," Slick said with a grin. "Admit it, we would have never found our way back to our Mystic Bay if it hadn't been for my new watch."

"Now wait just a second, you have to give some credit to my electric car. It worked, after all" Winky said with a hint of pride in his voice.

"It did not," said Slick. "That has to be the lousiest electric car I've ever seen. It was a good time machine, but a terrible means of transportation."

"How can you say that?" Winky asked .

"We never left your backyard, let alone Mystic Bay!"

"You're right, and I am going to fix it so that no one else ever gets trapped in time like we did," Winky said. He disappeared into his dad's garage.

When Winky returned, he was armed with a huge sledgehammer. Slick knew what Winky was going to do and said nothing. The world wasn't ready for time travel. He watched as Winky turned their time machine into dented scrap metal and black plastic chips.

Slick was so busy celebrating their successful journey home that he had forgotten all about his dad's train transformer. "I hope my dad doesn't get a sudden urge to play with his trains." He sighed.

"Oh, man; I forgot all about your dad's train transformer," Winky said. "He's going to be furious when he sees the mess in his basement."

"I don't care," said Slick. "That transformer might have carried my dad and his train set back to that swamp filled with dinosaurs if he turned it on."

"That's right," Winky said. "Nothing happened to us until I switched on your dad's train transformer. The lightning bolt that struck the oak tree must have melted its circuits in your dad's transformer."

"For some reason, that doesn't make me feel any better when I think about my dad's train set," said Slick. "Are you sure that it was the lightning?"

"Yes, we built an accidental time machine," Winky said. "We probably couldn't do it again if we tried."

"You know, there's something else you forgot to remove from our time machine before you smashed it into little pieces," Slick said. He turned pale at his next thought. "I hope you didn't change the future."

Winky slapped himself on the forehead. "Rats, Verne's battery! I forgot all about it." He tossed the sledgehammer down on the grass. "I don't think we can glue it back together

"What are we going to do?" Slick asked. "It will take us years to save up enough money to replace that battery. I'll be an old man in my twenties before I can afford to buy another candy bar down at *Dingledorf's.*"

"That's it!" Winky said. He ran into his house.

A few minutes later, Winky returned with an envelope, a pen, and a roll of masking tape. Slick said nothing, but followed his pal down to the pier. Winky figured out a way to pay Verne for the battery. With a little luck, the future would remain unaltered, too.

Once the boys reached the orange tractor, Winky scribbled Verne's name on the envelope and pulled the winning lottery ticket out of his pocket. Next, he placed the ticket inside the envelope and tried to tape it to the empty battery rack. The tape refused to hold, though, and the envelope simply fell to the ground.

The battery's frame was rusted from years of exposure to the bay's salty air. Tiny flakes of rust covered the sticky side of the masking tape. Winky tried taping the envelope to the frame three more times, and each time it fell to the ground.

"It won't stick to the frame," Slick said. "Somehow you've managed to alter the future so that masking tape no longer sticks to anything."

When Winky glared at him, and Slick decided that it might be in his best interest to shut up. After a few minutes, Winky came up with the idea of constructing a huge loop out of tape and attaching both ends to the envelope. Then, he hung the envelope around the battery frame, just like an ornament on a tree. This time, it remained in place.

"There, that should buy Verne a couple of tractor batteries." Winky laughed.

Then Winky heard a familiar voice—one that Winky had been hoping not to hear. The boys were standing too close to his tractor, and they looked guilty.

"Don't even think about running," Verne said as he finished helping Elgin tie up his patrol boat.

"Hi, Verne," Winky said. "Were you out on the bay?"

"Don't give me that innocent look," Verne said. "You two had to be involved."

"I don't know what you are talking about," Winky said. "What were you doing down by the pier?"

"Helping Elgin and looking for my battery," Verne said. "Both of you, empty your pockets. I want my battery back. Where is it?"

Slick was about to admit his part in the battery kidnapping when he was spared by another familiar voice.

"Now what did you lose, Verne?" Cole Schooner, one of the local firemen, asked the old farmer.

"Verne's looking for his stolen tractor battery," Elgin explained to Cole. "Verne is convinced that Winky and Slick were in on the daring caper."

"So?" Cole asked. "What's the problem? They either took it or they didn't."

"Verne is making both Winky and Slick empty their pants pockets to see if they are hiding his tractor battery in their trousers," Elgin said.

"Verne, you know can't fit a tractor battery into a pair of jeans," Cole said. He spotted the envelope dangling beneath the tractor. "Look here, Verne, someone left you a note on Betsy's battery frame."

Verne opened the envelope and took out Winky's lottery ticket. The old farmer looked back inside the envelope, hoping to find a note explaining why his battery was missing. The envelope was empty, except for the ticket.

"I thought you were going to explain everything in a note," Slick whispered to Winky.

"I forgot to get paper when I was inside my house," Winky said. "I can't remember everything."

"Maybe we should tell Verne what happened and why we took the battery," Slick said. "I'm going to tell him how the lightning bolt turned your electric car into an accidental time machine. And wait until we tell Verne how we took care of that giant dinosaur."

"Everyone will think we're crazy and then probably lock us up forever," Winky said. "No one is ever going to believe that story. Just keep quiet."

"Get a load of these numbers." Verne laughed. "2, 4, 6, 8, 10, and 40. Now that is a losing lottery ticket if ever I saw one. No wonder they didn't leave me a note; they were probably too embarrassed to admit that they picked those numbers."

He tore the winning lottery ticket into teeny tiny pieces, and then tossed them into the bay. Winky and Slick looked on. The future had definitely not been altered. And the boys realized that peeking into the future to win the lottery was probably considered cheating, anyway.

"You can have the battery from my patrol boat, Verne," Elgin said. "It's due for a new one. You can't be caught out on the bay with a weak battery. That boat has to start every time."

"Ten-four, good buddy," Verne said with a big smile. "Now, I'm kind of glad they took my battery. Thanks, boys; you did me a favor. I owe you one."

"How did he know it was us?" Slick asked Winky.

"He doesn't," Winky said. "And he won't ever know unless you start blabbing."

"I'm keeping my mouth shut," Slick said. For once, Winky was convinced that he would.

"Why don't we all go fishing? Cole suggested. "I feel like going out on the bay. It's beautiful out right now, and there aren't any storm clouds on the horizon."

"Ten-four, good buddy, ten-four," Verne said and climbed aboard Elgin's boat before anyone had a chance to change their minds.

"Can we go fishing, too?" Winky asked. "I missed the fish smells and the bay breeze."

Slick gave Winky a sharp look. Luckily, no one else found anything strange about his comment.

"Sure, there's enough room for all of us on board," Elgin said.

The five residents of Mystic Bay quickly boarded the patrol boat now that it was off duty. Next, Elgin allowed Verne to fire up the motor. Cole got ready to cast off the bow line. Winky and Slick tossed the stern line into the bay.

It felt good to be back in a world where you could feel the wind blowing against your face. Winky could smell the fish that were left stranded on the beach at low tide. Seagulls called to one another as they hovered over the boat and waited to be fed.

Just as they cleared the pier pilings, Scooter called out to the boys. He didn't want to be left behind. Life was more exciting with Winky and Slick.

"Hold everything Verne; here comes Scooter," Elgin said. The beagle leaped onto the deck. "Alright, Verne. Hit the throttle."

Scooter gave Winky a sloppy kiss as they headed out to sea. Then, he selected a spot next to the boat's anchor and curled up to take a snooze. Occasionally, a seagull would land on Elgin's deck and venture too close to the lifeless body. That's when Scooter would suddenly spring to life and lunge at the helpless gull.

It was a sunny day out on Mystic Bay with the sun hanging high in the sky. The men fished while Winky and Slick kept glancing nervously up at the sun. The boys were beginning to get nervous. It hadn't moved.

Only when Winky and Slick were convinced that the sun had climbed a little higher in the sky did they relax and finally cast a line out into the bay.

While he fished, Winky thought about what he had been through. He thought back to their narrow escape from the dinosaurs, and made a mental note to check out that photo he snapped of the mysterious rock. He thought about the distant future and shuddered, vowing to take care of Mystic Bay before bubble houses became necessary. Then Winky couldn't help but wonder if that old couple he saw living in his house of the future were really his parents. He never saw their faces, so he couldn't be sure.

Winky was a little nervous to go home that evening. What if the old people were still living in his house? What would his mother say? And how would he explain why they were there in the first place? Fortunately, Slick came to his rescue before he blew out a brain cell.

"Winky, look," Slick said and pointed up in the western sky. "The sun is beginning to set, and it isn't moving too fast or too slow. Everything is back to normal."

"I hope you are right about that," Winky said.

Slick tossed his only catch back into the bay. For now, he was content to watch the sun set as they headed back to shore. White foam chased their boat and gradually spread out across the water.

Winky joined Slick back by the stern. From there he watched the white foam slowly take on a pinkish hue as the sun continued to sink ever so slowly into the bay. You could almost hear it sizzle when it made contact with the ocean.

Seagulls and other birds disappeared from the sky over Mystic Bay, searching out a place to roost for the night.

"Are we going to build another time machine?" Slick asked. "I'll let you use my watch for parts."

Winky thought about Slick's question for a moment before replying. He reflected on their adventure, and how it all started.

"If I ever build another time machine, it will be purely by accident," he said.

The patrol boat docked, and Elgin announced that it was time to go home.

"Okay, you two," Elgin said. "Get off my boat. It's way past your suppertime."

"You can say that again," Slick said.

Winky just laughed.

Watch the entire *Winky Studmire* series unfold at:

**WinkyStudmire.com**

Winky and Slick always try to reply to their friends, so be sure to "like" **Winky Studmire** on Facebook and leave your own comments on their posts.

Check out Winky's latest photos and puzzles, and share the fun with your friends.

Who knows? Maybe you could be part of Winky's next adventure!

# ABOUT THE AUTHOR

G.T. Wiley lives and writes in Western Pennsylvania.

For a complete list of his books, please visit:

**www.byrnepublishing.com**